The Healing Soil	1
The Retreat	10
Garrotted	16
Siem Reap	19
Phnom Penh Lakeside	24
Sihanoukville	30
Estate Agent	42
Sex text and ATM	49
Unplanned Encounter	54
Life Time Visa	60
Guns, dogs, and Russians	68
Headline News	71
Entrapment	75
Back in Sihanoukville	84
Kampot	90
At my doorstep	95
The Minister of Culture	101
Blank Canvas	106
Two visitors	113
A visit from Don	119
The Hit List	127
Accomplices	133
A Welcome Addition	139

Crystal Meth	142
Dark Web Idea	149
Ned and Chuck	160
A display Trophy	164
The Network	171
Juno and Hana	178
The Middle East	182
Live Streaming	185
Reconnected	192
In the Name of God	198
River Boy	210
The Keffiyeh (Arabic Headdress)	213
Not part of the plan	218
The Worldwide Web	227
Don in Korea	232
Spirits Reunion	239
A New Beginning	242
Acknowledgements	247

THE DIARY OF A SAFFRON ASSASSIN

LAUCHLAN CAMPBELL

Copyright © Lauchlan Campbell 2023

All rights reserved.

No part of this publication may be reproduced, distributed, or transmitted in any form or by any means, including photocopying, recording, or other electronic or mechanical methods, without the prior written permission of the publisher, except in the case of brief quotations embodied in critical reviews and certain other non-commercial uses permitted by copyright law.

THE HEALING SOIL

In the early morning at the fringes of the Thai-Cambodian border, I stood as a silent silhouette against a tapestry of travel and trade. The air hummed like a Buddhist Mantra with the wearied steps of those Cambodian traders returning to their homes. I could see their facial expressions that they couldn't erase the horrors of the past, each carrying stories in their mind and weighted bags they clasped tightly in their hands. I also carried a load in the recesses of my tormented psyche – a history of violence and trafficking drugs, of prison in China – for crimes I did commit – and a childhood of silent screams. My depleted spirit ached for something good as it ran towards my future. Here, on this tattered edge of a land scarred by history's cruel hand, I was hopeful that my pilgrimage of peace would sow the seeds of a brighter future. How wrong I was to be.

Arriving at the border of Thailand and Cambodia the immigration and customs procedure was quick this was due to a few selected local boys from the Cambodian side who had been allowed into no man's land to help travellers carry luggage. I knew of these unofficial jobs supposedly allocated to help the new arrivals but had also heard stories of people's bags being rifled through. I decided to carry my own luggage just to be on the safe side. It was just before midday when I cleared immigration and customs and saw a gathering of travellers standing on the Cambodian side. My next thought was a place to eat and stay for the night. I felt like an immediate attachment like a magnetic field grounding me to the land. I could feel my tiredness and pain seeping from me onto this already aching soil. I felt that I could identify with their suffering but not on the scale those poor souls had endured. I pondered on how we measure suffering and couldn't find any conclusion. As individuals, it could have been a cut or broken bone but as a nation, it was too far beyond my limited understanding to make an assessment. I shared a transit van with five more travellers. I listened to their excitement as they took in the surroundings it was nothing new for me having passed through similar surroundings with my travels around Southeast Asia. I could feel that those young travellers probably didn't know about the horrific near genocide that had befallen the gentle-hearted people of this land. I could hear it from their constant chattering and wide-eyed expressions listening to them snigger while pointing out that the locals wore straw hats and torn faded clothing as they trudged through the muddied field with unharnessed carabaos beside them. I felt totally detached. I asked to be dropped off at a small town called Battambang.

As the bus trundled along bumping over potholes looking out of the window, I could see a clear blue sky and a welcoming heat from the sun as it beat down onto the window. The landscape looked serene. The tranquil colour of the cloudless blue sky in contrast with the rice shoots sprouting from the soil was inviting. There were platforms with palm leaf roofs on stilts spread across the fields for the farmers to rest out of the blistering afternoon sun along with scarecrows made from bamboo sticks black plastic bags and multi-coloured rags to ward off birds from eating the rice seed. The driver stopped on route allowing a couple of food and drink vendors to sell their products. The smell of fried spring rolls and sliced pineapple chunks was a welcoming opportunity to have a snack. The Killing Fields movie popped into my head - seeing that film left an indelible mark on my soul. The foreign invaders, the Pol Pot regime, and all the other horrific wrongdoings that this country had endured humbled me. I felt a hollowness inside and couldn't relate to my suffering anymore. It seemed that any misfortune I had endured was self-inflicted and not imposed upon me by other countries' invading armies or a despot dictator. A new awareness swept over me and now realised the immediate attachment that I had felt upon arrival. Listening to the other travellers brought me out of my muse, little did they know those tranquil surroundings they gazed upon were once fields filled with blood.

In contrast, this place would be my healing ground. The extraordinary suffering the people had experienced there made me realise how insignificant my past experiences had been in comparison.

The van stopped after a couple of hours at a market terminal we were surrounded again by vendors selling chicken and other foods, which I declined, having already eaten spring rolls on the van. We were immediately set upon by motorbike drivers, all offering their services.

I got out, along with another rather overweight guy, who seemed to be about the same age as me. He was sweating in the heat, his oversized polyester shirt sticking to his pallid, glossy skin.

He stretched out a rounded hand and said, "Hi, I'm Conrad, from the USA, do you want to share a taxi to a hotel?"

I was loath to touch him, finding both his clammy hand and grating American accent off-putting. "Hi," I said, shaking his hand. "I'm Loc, I'm from Scotland."

We checked into a guesthouse recommended by my new travelling companion, who told me in the taxi that he had been coming there every year since 2000. The main focus of his enthusiasm was a place called the Chicken Shacks and how readily available the women were and how cheap.

I knew of similar scenes from past travels and wasn't interested but nodded my head pretending to be paying attention to his every word. The name had caught my attention – so I asked why it was called Chicken Shacks.

Conrad explained it was where you go to select your lady or ladies, he grinned with a twisted front tooth protruding which gave him a devious look.

He said he could show me them so it was agreed he would knock on my room door at 7 o'clock that evening and we would set off to explore the area.

The guest house room was clean it had a shower and television. There was a dampness and blackened mould stains on the wall next to the toilet. Placing my luggage down I lay back on the bed thinking about the chicken shacks and what a strange name for a place to pick up women. I was having second thoughts about meeting Conrad but placed those thoughts in the back of my mind for now.

After resting for a few hours, I got up and took a shower. Conrad was on time. He stood dressed in blue jeans and cowboy boots. I put on multi-pocket shorts, a T-shirt and a pair of sandals. We went outside and jumped onto the back of two motorbikes. Conrad fixed the transport price and told them where to go – he clearly had done this many times before.

Battambang town wasn't fully electric and was still under construction. This was due to the influx of sex tourism and foreign business setups. This was common knowledge as news travelled fast in this part of the world which was notoriously known as one of the renowned sex markets of Southeast Asia. The bamboo scaffolding appeared to hang like the leaning tower of Pisa at every corner. There was a mangle of unconnected electric cables that appeared to look like the head of Medusa but instead of repelling evil, it appeared to my imagination to be inviting it in.

We started going down narrow dirt paths with only the bike light as a means to see. We eventually came to a stop at what I would describe as an illegal squatter's area. It was all temporary wooden structures with straw thatched-type roofs. There was electric light from generators run by gasoline compressors, so coloured flickering lights flashed like a go-go-style disco bar.

I noticed one large, well-lit, gated villa, off to the side of the road which seemed out of place amongst this hovel.

Just as I placed my feet on the ground the girls immediately flocked to me. A few of them seemed to know Conrad and surrounded him, so I let him lead the way. As I walked, hands started to massage my shoulders – so much so that I was relieved to be able to sit down, just to have a bit of distance from them.

The place stank of stale spilled beer and old cigarette butts from the overflowing ashtrays on the dirty tables.

Conrad started asking an elderly woman about some of the girl's ages.

She replied, "They are very young Sir."

Conrad then started to lift some of the girl's T-shirt tops saying, "I prefer it if the bitches haven't had pups yet – you can always tell from the stretch marks." Then without hesitation, he ordered us up two beers.

"I don't drink, thanks," I said, feeling sickened at his attitude towards these women, and he gave me a strange look.

I was feeling disgusted about the way this guy was treating the girls. I removed the girls' hands away who attempted to massage me my face showed the expression that I wasn't complying with their affections. Finally, I abruptly stood up and waved my hand angrily at the mamasan indicating I had no interest in consorting with the girls and she let out a burst of words. The girls left my side but were immediately replaced by other ones.

Conrad moved and visited another dilapidated den just fifty meters away so I went along. He seemed to want to explore the variety of girls available as there were several other huts nearby. I listened to his bargaining with the mamasan over a girl he wanted a short time with it was 15 US dollars and he wanted to pay $5. Conrad had touched her up and inspected her as you would maybe do to an animal before buying it at a cattle farm.

I thought this guy must be a sick-minded fuck and compassion wasn't in his mind. Lust was his master. I was about to lose control and wanted to batter the shit out of this moron. It was his touching and bargaining for sex with teenage girls, that had got under my skin. I took a deep breath reminding myself my journey to Cambodia was for meditation. The urge to punch this guy was difficult to control. The old character of my younger years where violent action came before thought nearly rose to the surface again. I stood up saying that I was tired and made my way back to where the motorbike guy waited.

Conrad stayed saying before my departure, with a grin, "You're missing a good time buddy."

I started to choke in a silent convulsion of emotional murderous rage but concealed it not wanting him to see my displeasure.

I lay in bed that night wondering what had brought on my anger so strongly. There was an urge to kill - right at the forefront of my mind. I had slept with many young women over the years in Asia but none were underage. I had certainly looked those sexy women up and down walking on the street and in the bars but there was something about how Conrad had inspected the young girls that annoyed me so much.

Prostitution is an age-old profession, not that I am justifying that trade but do find it acceptable if it is done by choice and not forced upon someone. I just could not believe that those girls were there by choice, living in a slum-like dump named *Chicken Shacks*. I didn't want to be involved in that scene. That was one thing I knew for sure. Even though the visual beauty of some of these girls could arouse me under other more humane circumstances.

The following morning, I awoke at 5 am, washed then went outside and walked the quiet streets. The early morning light was coming through and the air was fresh and clean before the day's traffic would pollute it.

I looked for a place to have some coffee so I could sit and contemplate the day ahead. So, I went into a baker's shop selling freshly baked bread and purchased two French baguettes. I asked, using hand gestures, for the whereabouts of a coffee shop and was directed to one just thirty meters away, on the opposite side of the street. Upon entering the establishment my eyes were drawn to porcelain figures of Chinese deities sitting on shelves around the walls. It turned out to be a pleasant morning drinking Vietnamese coffee and speaking Mandarin to the proprietor. I hadn't spoken much in the past few years and was testing my skills once again since leaving that country.

The old man was delighted and complimented me on my use of his language. I sat for a couple of hours and he gave me his brother's name card and suggested that I visit him in Vietnam if I ever went there. The old man offered me a job as an English teacher and even asked me if I would like to have a wife. That is incredible was the only thought that came to mind.

I had just arrived in Cambodia and had been offered a wife and a job. It can be exhilarating for the spirit to meet people who see you as an equal. I also knew well it was a financial opportunity for him. If I took the job or accepted his proposal about the wife it would have mutual benefits for us both.

I found in my travels that when you speak with Chinese people they respect and trust you a little more knowing you have taken the time to learn their language. Little did they know that I had learned the language in a Chinese prison – doing 15 years for drug smuggling. I had spent years travelling the world from one place to another. It was when I arrived in Hong Kong on New Year's Eve in 1979 that my travels took another turn from sightseeing to smuggling. I had run short of money and met up with a group who were involved in smuggling gold and technology to South Korea and India. I was financed by a syndicate who were smuggling gold. My first trip was to India, I took it upon myself to add cannabis resin to my list upon my return. I could sell that in Hong Kong which had a large ex-pat community. It was this decision that eventually became my downfall.

That is another reason that travelling can be so rewarding you can have many opportunities wherever you may happen to stop. Then again, I should mention that there are opportunist greedy traders and other hustlers with no good intentions you come up against daily so one has to watch one's step.

Thailand had made getting business visas and resident papers very strict in the past few years. Their new visa requirements were that you could only stay there for three months thus, resulting in the near impossibility of running a profitable business. There was no other option unless you had a Thai business partner or Thai wife. Therefore, the shift of small-owned foreign-run businesses such as nightclubs and street bars were moving into Cambodia, where at the border for a small fee of one hundred US dollars you could get a one-year renewable visa. That opportunity had started the invasion of foreign businesses into Cambodia, some of which were truly legal but very many were shady.

DIARY OF A SAFFRON ASSASSIN

The main reason that I had come to Cambodia was to go to a Buddhist meditation retreat for ten days. After that, I was planning to meet up with an old friend from Scotland named Don.

I had arranged to visit the Buddhist meditation retreat via the internet after making inquiries from my old friend Mike whom I had met in South Korea in 1980 and who was now a practicing Buddhist monk travelling around Vipassana centres in South East Asia and the Indian subcontinent. I needed to sit in silence and introspect after sliding into drug abuse back home in Scotland. My life was like a roller coaster going up and down confused and often over-emotional. I had spent most of my early life going from one institution to another, beginning with state-run childcare homes to state-run reform schools and prisons.

I thought for once that instead of being put into institutions I would voluntarily put myself into one but to introspect hopefully to finally find some direction in my life. I had previously experienced many nights of introspection whilst in prison – but lacked the power to take any action then. I had intentions to better my future - but by the following morning, I was back in amongst the madness and was surrounded by jail talk negativity.

The prison environment had a cloud hanging over it and very seldom does that cloud evaporate. The only opportunity for peace is at bedtime. I would sometimes lay in bed drifting back to my childhood. I recalled a song I heard in Bible class when I was a boy. Running over, running over, My cup is full of Running over. This was to show that the spirit of the Lord had filled your soul – in my case, it spilled over into dark waters leading down the wrong path to redemption.

I needed to be able to sit in silence away from the turmoil of daily life. I didn't want the temptation with the availability of alcohol and drugs. It was my decision to extract myself from society, meditate, and keep a calm state of mind regardless of what situation I found myself in.

THE RETREAT

The morning had arrived for me to enter the meditation retreat. I took a motorcycle ride; the driver handed me a brochure and pointed out certain locations on the route. They were sites of the killing fields showing mass graves. There was one photo in particular that caught my attention it was a pyramid of skulls. There was also a museum and he pointed to it indicating if I would like to visit them. I declined the offer but kept it in mind for the journey back. I didn't feel any need to get closer to death.

I arrived at the monastery, which was located in the countryside. It was a new day. A new and optimistic beginning. The air was crisp and the light of the morning sun filled me with hope. As I walked up the pathway, I looked at the surroundings it was a spacious area with lush greenery and coconut palms. I knelt down beside a man-made lotus pond running my fingers through the water reeds. I uprooted one smelling the flower inhaling deeply through my nose taking a breath of life into my lungs on this sacred land.

I gave my details to a young French lady who had told me she had been there for the past six months. She then showed me to my sleeping quarters. It was a small, whitewashed room, bare of anything but a bed and mosquito net. I laid my bag down and sat on the hard bed. I got the immediate feeling of restricted confinement and it wasn't pleasant. I wanted to breathe in that crisp fresh air and the scent of the flower just as I had done upon entering the premises. I then went walking outside and looked around the grounds and met two other guys who had just arrived. I introduced myself and they did likewise - one was from Finland called Jup and the other was a young Cambodian called Bong.

The young Cambodian man spoke fluently in Afro-American rap and had all the hand and body moves to go with it. These two guys informed me they had been living in Bangkok for the past couple of months having fun partying and had come here for some rest and recovery. The young Cambodian guy came from a very well-to-do family and his parents immigrated to the USA where he was born.

"Do you smoke pot old man," the young rapper asked.

"Occasionally," I replied.

" Let's go," he nodded and we exited the premises.

We walked a few hundred meters into fields and came out at a clearing where a massive Buddha head was carved on a rock face. It was supported with a mangle of bamboo scaffoldings around it.

Bong was quite an appropriate name for this young guy. He called over to someone who came out from a wooden shed next to the rock carving. Bong spoke with the man and within a minute had a bag of weed and a bamboo pipe. The surroundings were rugged and unkempt with long grassy clumps, and a few trees scattered around. Some large stones shaded part of the area, so we sat down in that cool spot.

It was excellent quality marijuana and before we realised it, we had been chatting like songbirds and were as high as kites. We drifted back to the retreat and I went to my room and lay down – far more relaxed now. I slept immediately, knowing the meditation schedule was at 4 a.m.

The next morning a gong echoed around the compound which was our sign to get out of bed. We all began walking to the meditation room and sat on the floor.

The classes were held by an Indian teacher but he was not actually present, instead, it was recorded on tape. Sitting with my eyes closed I followed the instructions which was to watch the rise and fall of my breath so that my mind wouldn't get caught up in other outward distractions and to always return to my breathing if it did. The voice of the teacher went on and on. The sound was disturbing and gave me a feeling of disorientation.

What was I doing there listening to a recording that was coming from a machine – and why was it haunting me? I took a slow breath to control myself repeating 'Om Mani Padme Hum'. A mantra that teaches you to transform your impure body, speech, and mind.

It reminded me of being in jail in China but I couldn't get out of there because of the iron bars on the windows. Yet here I was doing it voluntarily. The session ended and returning to my room wasn't feeling good my entire mind was flooded with negative thoughts. We all went outside after resting for one hour and began a walking meditation. We then sat again listening to the cassette for two more hours then returned and waited our turn to take a cold wash from buckets left inside the toilet area.

The food was served that evening, which consisted of rice and vegetables. I ate hungrily as the portion was sparse. Returning to my room and sleeping restlessly until the following morning's wake-up gong. Going to the meditation room my only thoughts were 'What in the hell are you doing here?'

I had met a woman called Linda, with her husband and family, in Thailand – and something Linda had said was ringing in my ears. Their final destination was New Zealand they had sold everything and planned to immigrate. I had told them my plans about going into a monastery. Linda had said to me, "It would be better if you didn't go, but instead stay outside and help others." Now thinking back, her advice was good. The rest of that day was a repeat of the previous one I wasn't connecting with my surroundings.

The following afternoon at the retreat I decided to visit the lady whom I had met upon arrival and let her know how uneasy my feelings were and that I was going to leave. During the registration into the retreat, several questions were asked and had to be filled in. One question was do you have any psychological problems? I had now realised that my intention to come to Cambodia was more deep-rooted than I had first thought. There was that immediate magnetic grounding I had felt. 'What was I doing at the retreat anyway? Looking for what?' I asked myself.

The young lady assured me it was not any problem at all and she wished me well when leaving.

I packed my bag walked out of the monastery and headed directly into the killing fields that the motorbike driver had pointed out to me. It was located not too far from the retreat grounds. Once there I sat under a tree looking up at the sky then got up and went to a nearby hill where human skulls were piled up in a cave like an Egyptian pyramid. I stared into the skull's hollow eyes, then reaching over, touched one.

The immediate feelings that invaded my soul came from the skull this was a child raped and then murdered. I had a flash of visions of dark shadows entering a village. I heard the screams of children. I saw the shadows chopping at bodies I heard gunfire. It was mayhem all around. The face of a little girl looking at me with terror in her eyes as she lay naked and bloodied on the ground.

I got out of there quickly; this spirit was very angry and there was a distinct feeling of revenge. The smell of fear and anger left a bitter taste in my mouth. The skull radiated a dead decayed matter that left a distinct mark on my psyche like indelible ink.

I walked back to the dirt road sat on the ground and waited. When a motorcycle came along, I waved it down and headed into town. On the journey back, my head was filled with a reddish haze feeling detached and with sudden bitter bile in my stomach. I kept looking over my shoulder having that feeling of being followed.

I arrived back at the guest house and took a shower, drying myself in front of the mirror. As I looked into my reflection a little girl was standing beside me. The bile I had felt in my stomach at the cave rose into my mouth. I spat out a dark green gooey substance onto the floor. I wiped my face with the towel in shock. She reached up her hand and took told of mine and I could feel the small fingers wrapping around my palm.

With a start, I turned my head and looked down but there was nobody there.

I hadn't even smoked a joint and shook my head in bewilderment. I would stay another night at the same guest house in Battambang avoiding any possible meetings with Conrad to whom I had acquired a sickening dislike.

That evening walking along the main street it was just hustling with pimps trying to sell me sex and drugs. The sound of those persistent voices spoken with annoying broken English was grating

"You like young girls sir, very nice sir, you have look, sir, very beautiful sir."

I ignored all the offers and continued walking through a small market area. I stopped to buy a dragon fruit and ate it whilst strolling along. I saw a large billboard in bold lettering.

Underage sex is a criminal offense.

There was a poster of a man holding a little girl by the hand walking down an alley with their backs turned pain gripped across my chest like a mountain climber's grapple hook. The activity of a developing town was all around but there was also a sense of desperation - a pulse in the air – that I couldn't put my finger on.

Having come out of the monastery earlier than planned, I decided to purchase a ticket to visit Angkor Wat in Siem Reap before meeting up with Don. I walked back to my hotel and sat awhile thinking of the surroundings in this town and how nice it was but for the constant hassle from motorbike taxis and human flesh for rent or sale hustlers. It could spoil your day listening to the constant offers of sex and what got me even angrier was it was their people and even their children they were trading.

I informed the receptionist; that I would be checking out the next morning then went to bed early. I didn't have a good night's sleep, a rare occurrence for me as I had always slept soundly most of my life. I had spoken with a young guy at the desk asking him about places to stay near Angkor Wat he told me many nice places sirs, my friend can meet you, sir, what is your name sir? I wrote my name on a piece of paper and gave it to him.

Whilst eating lunch the previous day I was transported back to Scotland and found myself with that group of ex-criminals in Glasgow, at a place called the Gang Hut. Remembering what one of the guys had said during crossed conversations. Loc you should murder that bastard pop star paedophile when you go back out to Asia. I hadn't picked up on his comment at the time but now a year or more after it had resurfaced.

GARROTTED

I had bought some Chinese fortune cookies whilst at the coffee shop then after reading about my supposed future good fortune placed the waxed wrappers on my dressing room table.

As I lay in bed that night going over my encounter with Conrad my thoughts were caught in a crossfire. I got out of bed and sat in the lotus position closed my eyes and took in long slow breaths. My mind couldn't be calmed. It drifted from one thought to another. The constant reoccurrence that came to the forefront was about the spirit girl and her suffering. I decided the problem was people with the same detachment from compassion as Conrad had displayed at the Chicken Shacks had to be confronted and dealt with. It was against the teachings of the Buddha but the thoughts were too powerful to control – as my actions would also be to follow. With intense clarity, I knew I had to eliminate him.

I wrote out a mantra covering the wax paper over it and then rolling it into a ball before placing it into the folds of my robe. I had made the conscious decision to put an end to this predator's life. I put on my robe to appear like the monks who rose early in the morning to go into the streets to collect alms. It seemed appropriate at that moment in time, and I knew I would need to fit in with my surroundings upon my departure from the hotel. Monks' eyes always faced the ground when collecting alms this would assist me in not being recognised as a foreigner when entering back onto the streets. I figured myself blending in with the orange flow steadily passing by.

It was 5.30 am and I felt that I was on autopilot being guided by the spirit girl. I felt her tiny hand brush upon the hair on my leg and it took my mind back to my childhood. I had felt this sensation before only it was the leg of a hairy man forcing himself upon me. I immediately pushed those thoughts away my focus now was to not allow this heinous abuse to be put onto other children.

I then went downstairs and quietly turned the handle on Conrad's room door but it was locked. I stood there thinking of what to do next. I knocked on the door and waited but didn't get any response. As I was about to depart, Conrad opened his door sleepy-eyed with an expression of surprise on his haggard face.

I forced a friendly smile on my face and said, "I'm sorry to disturb you, but I'm leaving today and wanted to say goodbye." Before he could say anything, I was already entering his room.

Conrad still in a sleepy daze just looked at me.

I walked towards him pushing him back further into the room.

It was all so sudden he fell backward onto the floor.

I immediately pulled the rope from my robe and wrapped it around his neck then rolled him on top of me his face looking upwards then began to strangle him. I could smell the stale stink of cigarettes and alcohol on his breath.

Conrad struggled kicking his legs. His hands desperately tried to free his neck from the tightening rope. I continued to garrotte him until the last gasp of air came out of his abusive mouth. I got up from under him and saw that bloodstains from his neck wound had come through onto my robe. I was disgusted by the sight of this man his sperm-stained underwear still with a fishy smell of sex clinging to them. Bile rose into my mouth and I spat it onto his groin.

I held the Mantra pulled his stained underwear down and pushed it up his butthole. I wanted to demean him the way that he had done to others. While this despicable man lay dead on his back, clasping my hands I bowed my head and said, "See you in another life you fucked up scumbag." I didn't feel anything my mind and body were totally detached it was surreal in many ways. I had just killed another human being. I didn't know if I felt angry or guilty it was all so sudden and hadn't the time to give it any thought. In my shocked state of mind, I had still come to the realisation that had to leave this hotel without bringing attention to myself.

I then took off my robe, and underneath I wore a t-shirt and a pair of khaki shorts. I punched his already dead head before leaving the room. I didn't feel any sense of regret or compassion.

As I was exiting the premises I turned around and could see a reflection in the guesthouse window of the little spirit girl. She looked down at me this time with a smile on her face.

I joined the steady stream of monks who were on the street collecting alms there was a calm that had returned within me. My quest for spiritual liberation was depleted, having failed by killing and violating another human in the most distasteful way. And yet, the release of violent energy, as well as the knowledge that Conrad would never again hurt another child, filled me with elation.

I could feel the child spirit at my side, she was pleased with me but wanted me to know that we were only getting started. She was giving me the scent of retribution, for the other abused children, not yet having been revenged. This was not a friendly spirit and she was still not content.

I was somewhat conflicted with what I had done - surely, I was now attached to the wheel of life and death and definitely would be reincarnated into some other hell.

Even then I had this feeling that I had started something I would not be able to control or possibly stop.

SIEM REAP

The journey to Siem Reap was by riverboat. I was looking forward to visiting the seat of the Kymer Kingdom. I was impressed by photos I had seen of the 8th Wonder of the World Angkor Wat Temple. The boat held about 40 passengers many of whom headed to the upper open deck myself included. The trip took six hours mostly passing by uninteresting water reeds. It did have a few scatterings of river houses with the children diving from their homes into the water laughing and shouting greetings to tourists. I didn't have a camera or any interest to take photos but there was an incessant clicking all around me. I still had some marijuana that Bong had purchased for me on the first day we met outside of the retreat.

Laying back I lit a joint - having prepared a few the night before.

A lady interrupted me from my muse, smiled, and said in accented Italian English, "Good smell."

I replied, "It is a better taste," and handed the joint to her.

That started the conversation she told me her two friends travelled every year to a new destination and had been doing so for many years. I was impressed at all the countries they had travelled to. They were all in their late forties and successful intelligent women. A few others on the roof deck wanted to participate in smoking. I handed out some joints, then went inside to the toilet and rolled a few more. We had a little gathering and exchanged travel tales while the boat movements rocked steadily and the wind cooled us. Although there was a relaxed atmosphere during the journey. In the back of my mind, I felt that getting closer to the ancient city would give me insight into the people of this land. The magnetic feeling, I had for the soil upon arrival in Cambodia was somehow like two north poles and I was now being disconnected.

It made me think about Conrad had my actions offended the spirit of the soil and disowned me.

When we disembarked, I saw someone at the pier holding a sign written in large print, 'Welcome Mister Loc'.

I couldn't imagine who could know I was there. So, I spoke to the guy and asked him how he knew my name.

"Sir," he told me, "Your friend at the Battambang guest house had texted me to meet you."

Letting out a relieved sigh, I remembered my chat with the young receptionist the night before I had checked out. Fuck me, being stoned had brought paranoia over me, thinking I was being followed or watched.

He went on to tell me, "It is a free ride to the guesthouse, Sir."

The feeling of paranoia and looking over my shoulder was happening more frequently. I could sense it ever since touching that child's skull in the cave. Then again more vividly at the guesthouse, when leaving, that I was not alone. I wasn't sure if it was instinct or insanity that had entered my psyche but I certainly felt uncomfortable. I had fleetingly gone over what happened whilst on the boat. Did someone see me leaving the guesthouse premises? I was caught up in the moment of meeting new people my mind couldn't fully absorb what I had just committed. I hadn't made a well-detailed plan to kill Conrad and now began to think about the consequences of my action. We had both checked into the guesthouse together. We had taken motorcycles to the chicken shacks together. I had the feeling when the body of Conrad was discovered that the Police would want to question me.

I watched the other travellers being harassed by the motorbike drivers for a moment and then took the offer of a free ride to the guesthouse recommended by the previous place.

I hadn't got my backside on the seat of his motorbike when he asked me, "You want any dope, Sir? Do you want lady Sir?"

The word 'Sir' was annoying and I already felt the urge to slap him. God dammed imbecile using a respectful word like 'Sir' while trying to sell me a human being. I gritted my teeth so hard that my jaw felt like it was wired.

On the way, the driver kept turning his head to ask me questions but I didn't reply. The traffic was mayhem. There appeared to be no rules of the road there, the same had applied in Battambang.

When we eventually arrived at the guesthouse and after checking in, I dropped my bag and headed out for a walk.

I visited the National Museum and watched the stone carvers at work taking note of the beauty of Buddhist statues being sculpted.

There was a garden area to sit in and I sat there soaking up the heat that even infiltrated the shade - the reinvigorating warmth soothed my muscles and calmed my brain. Closing my eyes, I breathed in the warm air, surrounded by peaceful sculptures in their traditional style, and their eternal beauty.

I did not know much about Cambodian history only what I had read of Pol Pot and the killing fields. As I sat thoughts about being in the Chinese prison resurfaced – specifically after I had been transferred to a new jail outside of the city. I vividly recalled the Warden of the prison making a statement that Shanghai Qing Pu Prison was a modern civilized prison with a strong emphasis on cultural values. I had written a request to the relevant prison authority to be able to study art and this request had been granted.

By the time I left the museum, it was late afternoon and I searched the town for other artworks - in particular oil paintings on canvas. I intended to look at other artist's works to compare with my own. Sitting at the museum rekindled my artistic spark and I wanted to explore more.

I stopped at one artist workshop all around the walls and floor lay partly finished paintings of Angkor Wat in various seasons from sunsets to full moons and monsoon rains.

I didn't have much interest in purchasing any so I headed back to the guesthouse. On my return I stopped at a place to eat and enjoyed a vegetable curry with rice it was a good size portion and left me full and contented.

I had tried speaking with the woman serving the food but she didn't understand me or indeed spoke English at all. I noticed that only motorbike drivers, hotel staff, prostitutes, and drug and human flesh sellers spoke some English. Their vocabulary of course was limited to offering some sort of service mostly unlawful. It would be difficult to get around without communication but I would manage as I always had done on my past travels.

That evening sitting downstairs at the guest house bar I ordered a bottle of water. I saw a couple of men around my age they had their arms around two young Khmer girls and drinking Angkor beer. I felt a slight tightness gripping my chest. It was a similar situation as the Chicken Shack but with more, hygienic and decorative surroundings with a bartender and menu. The men openly fondled the girls and laughed over loudly. It was typical behaviour from an alcohol-induced state of false courage and bravado which irritated me. I was soon joined by two young ladies wearing short skirts well above the knee line.

They confidently sat beside me and said, "Hello mister," in soft sheepish voices I asked who had taught them to speak English but was given a vacant but somewhat charming smile in response. I then enquired further as to their age using my fingers to indicate my meaning.

One girl said she was 19, and the other said 22. I thought they looked younger than that.

After some time, other foreigners arrived and the girls deserted me. I sat eavesdropping listening to those guys asking questions. Their requirements amounted to having group sex. One of them said with no holes barred this of course went over the girl's head but it certainly didn't go over mine. The same guy then directly asked if they were anal virgins. I could see the confusion on the girl's faces they didn't reply. The urge to hurt those guys arose within me simply because of their crude language. I gave it some thought those girls were not underage. The voice of someone in my mind would say kill them then the voice of reason would say, "It is not your business you were supposed to come to Cambodia and become a monk." I could feel a coldness touching me then the spirit girl reminded me about Conrad but I managed to ignore her.

I was about to go up to my room to rest when a guest house worker sat down and asked me, "You like virgins, Sir?"

I just told the guy, "No maybe some other time," and went upstairs.

I had a dream that night and, in the morning, only recalled shadows in an alley, a light flickering with shades of orange, the poster **Underage Sex is a Criminal Offence** which I had seen in Battambang, and a scowl on the child's face I had touched in the cave.

PHNOM PENH LAKESIDE

I only stayed in Siem Reap for a couple of days then headed to Phnom Penh. I had overheard other travellers talking about Lakeside guesthouses and it sounded like a good place to lay back and chill out. I stayed at one near the lakeside called White River it was affordable for backpackers whom I liked to be around to hear the tales of their travels. I checked in laid my bag down then took a cold shower.

I shaved my head which I had done before going into the meditation retreat and had continued doing it. I then took a shower and selected some clean clothes. I had two saffron-coloured suits made from light cotton material whilst in Thailand. I had also bought a robe but I wasn't ordained. The loose-fitting trousers and jacket gave the appearance of being a novice monk so decided to wear one. I was sometimes asked by other travellers if I was a monk. My reply would be no I am not but had decided to apply the principles of the Buddha's teachings by serving the people on whatever path life put me on.

I had begun to notice that when wearing my saffron clothes, I didn't get as much hassle and none at all regarding sexual offers or hard drugs. The street dealers sold everything from crystal methamphetamine to heroin and opium that were unceasingly on offer.

DIARY OF A SAFFRON ASSASSIN

Sitting one afternoon in one of the waterfront cafes with a few other travellers smoking marijuana. It was tolerated in Cambodia and many coffee shops gave it out for free as a means to gather in customers.

I was quite at ease listening to the other travellers talk about places they recommended to visit until this skyrocketed French guy walked in. I could see by his fidgety movements and body language he was high on crystal meth which is a potent central nervous stimulant. I had watched a documentary about this drug - it was inexpensive to produce and caused havoc among the population in the country's lower classes. The effect of the drug was you couldn't sleep nor had any appetite for food. He had all the hallmarks of an addict - unshaven and dirty clothing.

He sat down beside us. I noticed that he had a cut above his eye and foam gathering at the side of his mouth. He leaned over and whispered in my ear, that he had good connections. He continued that if I needed kilograms of opium; he could get them for me. I looked him in the eyes and said, sarcastically "When was the last time you had a sleep Monsieur?"

The other people at the table told me to ignore him, that he had come a few times over the past few days. He would then be told to leave by the staff once he went too far annoying the customers. I considered myself a reformed drug offender who admitted that by my own choice was causing harm to my mind and body by smoking tobacco and marijuana but justified my decision by not selling addictive substances nor smuggling them anymore.

That evening I wanted to visit some nightlife changing my clothes and wearing a T-shirt. I didn't want to draw unnecessary attention to myself so the orange suit wasn't appropriate - it was like a traffic stop beacon light.

I went into the bar and ordered bottled water. The women were certainly desirable but I refused their offers on numerous occasions. It was tempting and made me think about how cheap life here is and how abundant sex was for sale. It was like shopping at the market. There was so much to choose from young women, ladyboys, and homosexuals parading by strutting in exaggerated feminine postures on the bar floor. At the cost of $10 to spend a night with any of these beauties depending on your preferences.

There was something inside me unsettling and still hadn't found the root source as to why yet. There was that soil attachment, which had rooted me upon arrival, and felt it was curing me of something.

I still had an unsettling feeling, similar to that when with Conrad at the chicken shacks. My head was full of past encounters reliving my personal abuses. I couldn't settle my thoughts. I was feeling agitated just being in the presence of this debauchery. Then recalling the boat trip, I had the feeling of being detached. My soul was in a downward spin one minute being connected to the land and the next being detached I felt caught in limbo. It was off-putting but didn't want to deal with it yet, something was going on in my mind and it would reveal itself in time. It was hypocritical that my thoughts and actions did not coincide with each other. It felt like I was a walking contradiction. Taking Conrad's life in Battambang seemed to be getting erased from my mind and replaced with the spirit girl congratulating me for taking action to eradicate the world of an abuser.

The following day, walking around, the town it was bustling with traffic. I visited the Russian market, it was named this because of the Russian expats living in that area of town. I saw fake designer gear in rows, alongside the market money changers, where the rate of exchange was slightly better than that of the banks. I took a seat at a market food stall and ordered noodles with a boiled duck egg and some unknown vegetables. The noodles tasted good.

As I sat there, I started reminiscing about meeting an old friend Don. Before I set out to travel to Cambodia, I had arranged to meet up with him. I had known him since my childhood days in Glasgow. Don had told me he would meet me at white sands beach in Sihanoukville. It was something we had discussed before I had left Scotland, and he'd said that if we missed each other we could meet up at Gordon's Coffee Shop - he had assured me it was a small town, telling me to" go each morning and he would be there. So that was the plan.

Don was a couple of years older than me he had got quite a reputation in the mid-1960s after a street gang fight on Tobago Street in the east end of Glasgow. It was a time when there were street gangs in every district in the city and beyond.

That specific fight was with a rival gang who had entered our area known as Tongland. This gang fight also resulted in clashes with the police. The Calton Tongs gang turned a police car over and then smashed it up. The following morning newspaper report headlined *TONG'S GANG GO ON RAMPAGE, POLICE STATION UNDER SEIGE*. There was blood spilled that night and Don was fully involved in the carnage.

Don was a man with a flare, he dressed immaculately, with a characteristic trait of often going to extremes to protect his family, along with a few selected friends. The one very clear characteristic was Don and the Calton Tongs gang had total disrespect for the law – to a point that bordered on insanity.

As the years passed and the gang life was put behind him, Don mixed with another crowd more focused on business and making money. He had become a property developer. I had been told due to his financial success he usually had a few hangers-on with no skills in life other than to massage his ego. When certain people had monetary problems, they turned to Don and some, unfortunately, took it for granted that when he bailed them out monetarily it was a free handout. The street rule in Glasgow in the circle we associated with kindness was certainly not a weakness. It was usually compassion and consideration for the mothers or wives whose husband or son was in jail leaving them less well off. In cases like this, Don did not expect any repayment. As to other cases of borrowing a loan was a loan and repayment should be made. If not, you would suffer the consequences which would usually result in a severe beating.

I had last met up with Don in the market cafe at a place in Glasgow known as the Barras. I had heard several stories about his success as a property developer and his continuous extravagant lifestyle. Upon meeting him one weekend at the market I could see awareness in his eyes and a concerned look on his face.

"How are you doing pal?" he greeted me. "When was the last time I saw you?" he inquired.

"Around 30 years ago," I replied

"Has it been that long?"

I could see by the shifting of his eyes that he was preoccupied with scouting the surroundings. We chatted about the past old gang days, but it was clear to me he had other things on his mind. He nodded to someone who had stuck their head into the cafe door and said to me that he had some business to take care of. Then he immediately slipped a bundle of folded banknotes into my hand. Before being able to say that I was financially ok, he departed saying that it was a little help since you have been away for a while and not earning. Then before exiting the café, he said, "Let's catch up again soon, you can find me every weekend here." and with that, he left.

I was out of touch with current affairs in the criminal underworld and could see Don was doing some sort of underhanded trade. I had no doubt Don would have a good reason for his minimum input that day.

Coming back from my reminiscing's I finished my noodles and headed back to the guesthouse. My appointment to meet up with my friend was fast approaching so it was time to move on. I bought myself a ticket at the guesthouse travel desk to leave the following day.

SIHANOUKVILLE

The bus journey to Sihanoukville was on the coast, and the road was bumpy but I was excited to be going to a beach again and to meet up with my friend. I had been told beforehand by another traveller of a place called the GST guesthouse which was around $5 a night and had internet access.

Upon arrival, I checked in and planned to go into the town the following day to locate the place my friend had mentioned, called Gordon's café - and hopefully link up with him. It was late afternoon and I walked from the guesthouse towards the beach, which was around 100 meters away. The sun caused me to shield my eyes and a little breeze rustled the coconut palms above me.

It wasn't long before being approached and hassled by motorbike drivers with the usual sales line of sex and drugs. Thinking to myself, 'Fuck, I haven't placed my feet on the sand and these sales pitches were already getting under my skin'.

I took off my sandals and strolled along the beach letting the waves splash onto my feet. The feeling of sand between my toes and an infinite blue sky with sunshine felt good. It was a busy beach with endless deck chairs filled by contented-looking foreigners and the flow of traders. I could hear the sounds of different music as it pumped out from the beach bars. One sign caught my eye it said, 'Free accommodation'. There was a bunch of young people hanging out eating, drinking beer, and smoking marijuana. I sat down listening to the music. It took me by surprise when hearing a Scottish group, The Sensational Alex Harvey Band song 'The Faith Healer' come on. It reminded me of when I took the train from London to Glasgow. I met the singer of the band on the journey to watch him play at an open-air concert at the well-known football ground at Celtic Park.

I was high on marijuana and in my altered state of mind thought it was a sign that this would be a more relaxing place to stay than the guest house. It was on the beach I could see the ocean and listen to good music.

I ordered a bottle of water and then asked about the free accommodation again. The young Khmer man introduced himself as Jai, and he told me that it was true and that would I like to have a look at the rooms.

I followed him to the back of the bar area. It was as basic as it gets, a row of wooden huts paper-thin walls, a bed with a mosquito net. The toilet and wash area were outside and very unhygienic so, I gave up on the free room offer.

I sat and spoke with Jai for a while he was selling bags of good marijuana for $5 a bag. I purchased two and asked if it was always available around here. Jai told me that even the cops sell it so don't worry smoking isn't a problem here. I looked around and could see a group of people with large rolling papers on the table. I went over to them and introduced myself then sat down to join in. It was good to be back amongst the mix getting to hear new travel tales and listening to their travel plans that often would never materialize but were told in all sincerity at the time.

At that table was one Indian guy from Delhi, one American guy, one Dane, one Swedish woman, and a Scotsman. It was not a bad collection of strangers to meet on a beach in Cambodia all having different reasons for being there. We chatted and smoked joints until sunset, a few other travellers had joined us and some had departed.

I left the beach with the vision haunting in my head of this young female spirit tugging at my shirttail. The Faith Healer lyrics pounding in my skull - was that a subliminal message or what? It seemed appropriate at that moment in time. *Your spirit doesn't have to grieve, all you have to do is believe*, the Faith Healer echoed in my head. I currently felt that my soul was grieving and needed healing.

.oOo.

The following morning, I went to Gordon's cafe around 10 o'clock. I spoke with a young Khmer lady who knew Don but told me that he hadn't arrived yet. I ordered an English breakfast just for the sake of having bacon, beans, sausage, egg and toast.

It wasn't long before the proprietor came out and said, "Good morning my wife tells me you are waiting on Don? he sat down and introduced himself as Gordon.

" Yes," I replied.

Gordon informed me that Don came most days the but the time that he got here depended on if he had a late-night drinking or had taken a woman home from the bar. Gordon then volunteered to tell me, with a wink of his eye, that my friend usually went home with a woman several nights a week. After that Gordon rejoined his young wife in the kitchen.

Don had told me the story that Gordon opened his coffee shop a few years back and employed this young 17-year-old girl to help him run it. Then one thing led to another and they became sleeping partners. As the story goes, the brothers of the girl came to the shop with an option which was he either marry their sister or pay them money. Don had told me that Gordon wisely and happily married the girl - and had a smile on his face at the opportunity (at 64 years of age) to marry the then nineteen-year-old Khmer lady.

As the saying goes money makes the world go around and poverty was abundant there so at the end of the day his young wife and family were now economically secure. I am not an expert on what people will do to secure a better life for themselves or family but it was obvious to me money was an important priority in this case.

Don hadn't turned up yet so after finishing my breakfast I left my room number with Gordon and took a walk around the town to take in the surroundings. Sihanoukville was a very small coastal town with two main tarmac roads. It was overcrowded with motorbikes and there were no pavements, so it was dangerous to walk in some places. I could see new construction going up all around and there was certainly a bustling atmosphere. Most of the tourist places were leased and run by foreigners who flew their nation's flag outside their premises. Another thing that I noticed was that most Western men were around my age or older. I was heading toward my 60th birthday and fitted in well enough. It seemed to be a place for the aged and retired but in fact, it was mostly for easy access to sex. I had just got here but had been soon educated more about the elderly movement. Whilst smoking marijuana at the Frog Shack the younger travellers had told numerous stories about the sex trade. Cambodia was full of mostly overweight foreign divorced men possibly looking for their second youth. It was a cheap lifestyle with inexpensive accommodations, low-priced food, drugs, and the availability of young women.

I got onto the back of a motorbike and headed to the beach and sat at Chamoi Frog Shack which was the one with free accommodation. Sitting down I ordered a Happy Shake; it is mixed fruits with marijuana. I decided to try one and a mango pancake to go with my order. I lay back on a deck chair and looked out at the water there were plenty of local children splashing around and playing with rubber tubing. The beach itself wasn't much to write home about, having a short sand area when the tide was in. I hadn't been there more than ten minutes when Don walked up to where I was sitting.

We immediately shook hands like two long-lost brothers being reunited. I told him my story about the monastery leaving out my experience with the spirit girl and the Conrad encounter. Don and I had discussed opening some sort of business in Cambodia whilst in the UK but now being here, the priority was to find a house to rent.

The both of us living in a hotel or guesthouse wouldn't do in the long run. Don had located a place called Snooky's, which was a Villa with a top floor for rent. The other half of the Villa was rented by an elderly disabled American guy called Mickey. Don suggested we go and have a look – and at first glance, we decided to take the place and moved in the following day. The cost of rent was $300 a month which worked out to $5 each a day – although it was the same price as the guesthouse I had found, it was a better deal than living out of a suitcase in a hotel room. There was a sign outside the house offering Vietnamese massage.

I was having breakfast downstairs one morning and spoke with the lady who managed the house She let me know the Villa was foreign-owned and she was the housekeeper. The owner and his wife were in Thailand on business.

My curiosity and groin were stirred by seeing the girls sitting in enticing provocative postures. I could see their legs widely apart and their underwear in full view. It certainly felt like an invitation. I asked her about the two stunning ladies sitting opposite me manicuring their nails. The woman told me they were Vietnamese and worked for her boss. If I wanted to have a massage or sex to let her know which girl I preferred. This clarified my first impressions regarding their enticing posture it was an invitation but not a spoken one.

Mickey had come out from his ground-floor room accompanied by another lovely young woman. The massage sign outside was a subtle way to offer what is known as massage plus or a happy ending which is short for being masturbated or full-on sexual intercourse. The housekeeper immediately sat down beside him and began to untangle a bunch of marijuana stems with thick buds swelling from them. My eyes popped open when she started to pick off some buds and roll joints for him. I sat there smiling thinking that's the way to start the day. Mickey called me over to join him then he went on to tell me stories of how good life here was.

Mickey went on to explain how much It would cost him only for medical treatment in the USA. He was being bathed and fed here plus as much pot as he could smoke. On top of that cheap cold beer to drink, along with any of the ladies to satisfy his sexual requirements. "I can't get that treatment in the USA," he smiled, "at least not for 600 bucks a month."

I looked over at one of the girls, she was stunning and oozing sexuality, smiling at me and blinking her eyes. The temptation and desire flushed to my groin but then the now-becoming familiar presence of that little girl's head in the cave of skulls reminded me of her presence.

I was momentarily transported back home again to the Gang Hut one early morning in Glasgow when high on chemicals.

.oOo.

It was typical Scottish weather for that time of year - a cold bleak winter day in late December. My mood was as heavy as the dismal sky outside my unheated abode in Glasgow. My soul had expired every last iota of psychic colour and my muse had discarded and abandoned me. After spending 12 years in Chinese jails from August 1991 until December 2003 on a cannabis conviction, songs such as Legalize it, and other cannabis promotional tunes still wafted through my somewhat disillusioned mind.

It was a rare occasion that one Friday evening I went to visit my brother's friend's house. My life was on a downward spiral pulling me into a vortex of depression. I had become a recluse of a sort very seldom leaving my house but I was now sitting amongst a group of men well associated with the harsh realities of prison life. It was an unusual atmosphere for me as I had lived in Southeast Asia and the Indian subcontinent for the past 30 years and was really out of touch with life in the UK.

I was accompanied by my brother Tommy who once was the leader of the group who had gathered this evening at a place known as the Gang Hut. It was a reunion of older heads most of them with adult and teenage children of their own. They sat smoking a variety of marijuana hashish and drinking beer whilst reminiscing past jail experiences and encounters with the law.

I enjoyed their company very much, but a lot of the humour was going over my head. The group talked about television programs I had never heard of the one they were laughing about was called *Still Game*.

Gathering by the jokes being made and by the current mental state that the others and I were in was caused by smoking homegrown Glasgrow Green. It was top-quality dried and cured cannabis buds with aromatic smells and exotic flavours of a fine homegrown weed. As I took in the surroundings there were posters scattered around the walls, one showing a group called MOJO Miscarriage of Justice organization.

There was a clenched fist holding barbed wire with the headline *Free the Glasgow Two* and other campaign banners. There was also one of the Scottish Socialist Party politician Tommy Sheridan advocating for an independent Scotland. It was a full wall collage combining posters of concerts such as Glastonbury, Redding, and numerous other music venues around the Country. It was a glimpse of past and happier days. ticket stubs, and rock n roll T-shirts, hung dust-laden across the room walls.

It was that night one of the gang Joe G said to me offhandedly, "Hey Loc you should go and murder that pop star paedophile out in Vietnam."

This was said as a side remark as he continued telling us about a documentary that he had watched on TV regarding the abductions of children for organ harvesting and prostitution in the sex trade in India.

We had all taken a small drink of what the guys called the mystery sip. It was a plastic sports bottle that was placed on the dining room table the ingredients after taking some was told it was a mixture of Cocaine, Ecstasy, Amphetamine, and LSD. I could feel the effects coming on rather quickly. As the night progressed the banter got louder. I sat mostly on my own, out of touch a little uneasy but feeling safe.

I left in the early hours of the morning. My brother offered to drive me home but I declined his offer and wanted to walk. I could use the early morning air to ease the tangled knots from my jumbled brain.

I walked slowly, my mind jumping from one scenario to another in vivid colours, before turning into a cloud of black and dark blue like the early morning sky above me. I took the route home heading up to Parkhead Cross then walked onto the London

Road passing my house in Calton. I continued onto Glasgow Cross then turned back up the Gallowgate en route back to my house. It was while walking past Baird's Public Bar that a voice in my head whispered to me.

It said I should go ahead with my plans.

As quick as the thought came it was gone stored away somewhere in my fragmented psyche just fleeting clicks in my drug-induced mind.

Go ahead with your plans flashed again and again. But I didn't have any plans.

Upon reaching my flat I still had waves of energy running through me. My focus kept returning to what Joe G had said during the conversation about child abduction in India. I could see pictures in my mind where children were kept in cages.

'Go ahead with your plans,' resurfacing again and again.

Once inside my house, I made myself a small pot of Chinese green tea. My flat decor was a mix-up of cultural relics collected over many years of perpetual travel.

I had sent them home for when or if I decided to live back in Scotland. My house painted an abstract picture of my character cultural schizophrenia that was my interpretation. My room reflected bits and pieces of me in no specific order. It was a sparse Japanese style of living, sleeping on the floor with a futon with no chairs to sit on but scattered Afghani multi-coloured cushions to lay back in comfort. On the wall hung a painting called Red Tape depicting a prisoner with his hands bound with red bondage tape reaching upwards into the infinite sky above him. I had done that painting whilst in jail in China. It was my interpretation regarding the communist bureaucratic system of never getting a final solution to complaints you made against the state.

I went into my bedroom stripped myself and now lay naked on the wooden parquet floor. I spread my arms and legs out to release some energy from my overheating body and brain. I didn't sleep at all tossing and turning with scattered thoughts and images of horror which got me through that ill-fated night.

It was in the early afternoon I got off the parquet floor my mind still groggy that I did my first paedophile search on the internet. I looked up the news story about the pop star arrested in Vietnam first, then began researching their habits and hangouts. I saw Cambodia, Philippines and Vietnam had been some of the countries these sex predators headed for. In an overwhelming surge of emotion, tears flooded my eyes reading about the abuses.

That early afternoon still looking at the computer screen I started to relive a childhood dream. I was hiding under a bed in a care home I had been sent to as a child. A large shadow of someone towered over me in a threatening manner. I had awoken from that nightmare terrified just before being caught but still with fear in my heart.

I wasn't sure if it was the drugs, I had taken but my heart mind, and soul were a twisted web of emotional pain reliving past horrid memories. I had the feeling that my insides had been gutted and was just a shadow peering into a computer screen. I was crying out the pain but not fully understanding why I was identifying so much with the suffering of others. I remembered the words go ahead with your plans but still didn't know what those plans were or what mission they were directing me towards.

.oOo.

As I sat at the table, I wasn't fully listening to Mickey I was preoccupied by past memories but I certainly felt the presence of an invading spirit and had done for a while now after my encounter at the cave.

I excused myself from Mickey's company stating I was going into town to do some shopping. I didn't yet have a sim card for my phone and in Cambodia, you needed a local person to sponsor you, plus showing your passport as full ID. I would ask Don about how he got around to doing that.

Don introduced me to one of his lady friends, we both got onto her motorbike and went into a mobile phone shop paying twenty dollars for the card and handed her the two dollars' commission that she had asked for. On the way back from the shop I could smell the scent from her hair and had a fantasy in the making.

On arrival at the villa, she asked me would you like a massage mister her use of English was okay and somewhat enticing. I asked how much to which she replied five dollars. I was thinking about where this will lead to, knowing what was on my mind. Lying on the bed fully clothed she told me to sit up and take off my shirt which I did then lay with my face on the mattress feeling her sit on my back and she started to rub my shoulders. I took a glance from the side of my eye she had white underwear on and I was getting aroused. I felt her explore my lower back with her knuckles and relief oozed from me. After paying her five dollars for what seemed hours of relaxing pleasure. I asked her name, and she told me it was Chua she was stunning and small in stature I could see her shape was lithe and agile with small protruding breasts.

"You like to have sex with me mister?" she asked.

My quick response was to speak to her in childish English. "No thanks. I am practicing to be a monk."

She smiled and rubbed my bald head then went downstairs to meet her friend.

I lay there thinking why didn't I take that wonderful opportunity? I then immediately felt my groin tingle with blood feeling aroused and at least felt assured I still could get an erection. It wasn't chest pains I was having now it was hot sweats and a pulsating groin. God was trying me or was it this little girl haunting me? Frankly, I did not know what was going on but it was certainly unsettling.

ESTATE AGENT

It was only after a few days of being there that the music from downstairs played by the Vietnamese girls started to annoy both Don and me. It was, after all, a business and the owners were currently in Thailand. I guessed with the boss not present the girls had free reign of the household. We both decided to look for our own place.

I had got hold of a real estate agent's phone number from a sign along the Ocheatuel Beach road and made a call. I was pleased to hear the person who answered the phone spoke English. I was given directions on how to find the place, which was next to the Vietnamese Embassy. I then phoned Don and we met up at Gordon's coffee shop then headed to the agency which was a five-minute ride on the back of a motorbike.

A young guy named Som met us and had a confident air about him that was refreshing. Som offered us water to drink and showed us a brochure of houses presently available for rent. It was decided we would go and look at one only a few minutes away from his office it was a three-bedroom bungalow. We arrived there it was a nice quiet location down a narrow street off the main road. We had a look inside but Don felt it was too small for two guys with not enough privacy.

The Villa next to it had a phone number and a sign on the gate for rent. We asked Som if he would call the number which he did. He said, "If you want to meet the owner, he will come now."

So, we decided to wait and within minutes the owner arrived.

After looking around that house we agreed on $350 a month with a one-year contract. On top of that, we were to pay cable TV 6 dollars a month plus water and electricity whatever we used, as it had a meter. We decided there and then we would rent it.

Don paid the first three-month rent in advance and the owner handed over the keys. We were both delighted from sharing the top half of a house at $300 a month to having our own five-bedroom Villa which had two levels and two entrances for $50 more - and this house was beautiful with a back and front yard. Don preferred downstairs which had two bedrooms' a shower toilet and a massive kitchen plus the lounge area was spacious also. I had the same upstairs only one room more and a veranda to hang my hammock.

Don had taken a liking to Som because he could inquire from him about business ideas and other possible business opportunities. Don handed him $50 in commission because the property we rented wasn't on his list but he did negotiate with the owner on our behalf.

Som was enthusiastic when Don asked if his boss would sell his company. Som replied he would inquire and phoned his boss there and then. After the call finished Som said his boss would like to meet.

Don told him he would be interested to talk and so it was arranged that he would go in the not-so-distant future and meet.

Don had already booked a ticket to return to Thailand and said he would contact Mr Chin - the owner of Angkor Real Estate - to discuss a possible buy-out upon his return.

LAUCHLAN CAMPBELL

.oOo.

Whilst Don was away back in Thailand I relaxed and got to know the area we were living in. One day I was laying out in the backyard of the Villa after having spent half the night at the beach watching fireworks displays. The beach had been decorated with a variety of sand sculptures with candles placed on and around them. It was quite a sight and local people sang and danced the night away while the foreigners either got stoned and drunk or more likely both.

Whilst laying out on a straw mat in the backyard of the Villa squinting my eyes from the afternoon sun, suddenly a lump of something fell onto the ground beside my head. I jumped up, startled, and thought it had been thrown over the wall from the house next door. I picked it up and saw that it was wrapped in a white plastic bag and tied tightly with duct tape.

I unwrapped the tape and upon opening it found $8000 in $100 bills. Trying to work out why it was thrown over our wall, panicking for a few minutes thinking someone might be setting me up. Paranoia lived with me, like my new spirit companion. Why would $8000 fall at my feet no way that could happen? There must be some underhanded motive. It was a setup, but by whom and for what reason?

Finally, I looked up at the window I had been laying under. I went into the kitchen and climbed onto the countertop - then I reached into the vent and came out with another wrapping.

My hopes for a great start to the New Year evaporated this time it was Hashish and keys and I realised immediately the bundle of cash belonged to Don. It had just fallen out of the vent where I had been lying.

I went into town that evening and sent Don an email explaining my good fortune and windfall. I made light of the situation and pretended that the God of good fortune had bestowed upon me his generosity.

I returned to the internet shop the next day, my friend replied saying he thought he had found a safe place to hide his money. Don asked if would like to come to Thailand, all travel expenses would be on him. I declined the free travel offer but did reply to loan me $1000 and I would return that money back to him at a later date. Don agreed and assured me not to worry or hurry with the return payment.

I knew Don well and he wouldn't be hassling me to pay back. Don also knew that I had a budget for daily living in Cambodia and taking a holiday to Thailand wasn't in it. I had saved money whilst working in Scotland but I had thought that I would be staying at a temple thus my cost of living would be low. In the email Don had also asked me to pick up some jewellery on route to Thailand and gave me the contact address.

I packed a small bag then headed out and bought the boat ticket for Koh Kong. It was a four-hour boat trip plus another one-hour jeep ride. I would be at the border that same day ready to cross from Cambodia into Thailand. Don had asked me to meet a Cambodian guy and spend the night at his guesthouse he had some business going on with him.

I arrived at my destination, checked in then went to the restaurant which was located on the ground floor. The guesthouse owner joined me at the table he shook my hand asking if I was a friend of Don. There was a desperation in his voice when he told me some plans regarding Don and himself buying land. I told him that my friend had not mentioned anything to me about buying land but asked me to meet up with him.

It was often personal questions asked when you spoke with many Cambodians male or female. It was questions like How much money do you earn? Do you have a pension? Are you married? Are you looking for a wife? And of course, with the shady ones do you want sex and drugs? This guy's line of questioning wasn't much different. Don had asked me to pick up a gold bracelet and precious stones he had paid to be set at a local jewellery shop here in town.

I went with the owner of the guesthouse and I collected the items. It was a beautiful piece of work and all handmade. I returned to the guesthouse and sat upstairs on the veranda and met a guy called Adrian whom Don had met the year before in Sihanoukville. Adrian had written a small book, which he had gotten printed, locally, and called it *'South East Asia IN YER FACE'*. I bought one from him, the usual price was $10 but he gave me one for $8 and signed it.

Adrian then told me about the cafe Freedom in Phnom Pehn and asked if I knew the owner a Scottish guy called Brian. I wasn't sure but did recall meeting a Scottish guy called Brian in Bangkok. Adrian painted a rather abstract picture in his description of Brian the crazy Scotsman. It seemed he had now lived in Koh Kong for the past four years and before that six or seven-year in Phnom Phen opening Cafe Freedom. Adrian told me that he had the best dope in town and carried a gun. Brian was said to have good connections and I could believe that after a decade of living here. Adrian gave me directions on how to get to his place - it was only a five-minute walk. So, I headed there. I arrived at his place and an Asian lady asked me if I was looking for Brian, nodding my head indicating yes.

"What's your name?" she asked as she dialled her mobile.

I told her my name was Loc saying I wasn't sure if Brian would remember me.

A moment later she handed me the phone and I said, "Hello Brian, you may not remember me …"

He interrupted saying, "Loc! I will be there in a minute pal."

About two minutes later a jeep pulled into the driveway and outstepped this guy with a large dog on a chain.

"Glad to see you," he said, "and how is your son Scott?"

Then it came to me, we had smoked dope together and smuggled around this part of the world for a long time. I knew him from Bangkok, he was doing the Golden Triangle trips to collect his weed. We started to talk about old tales. He had ended up in jail in Japan for two years and told me that he had gotten out of another drug smuggling case in Switzerland. He had now been married to a lady from Thailand for the past ten years, and he also had a son around that age.

Brian asked me to go out for a drink and when I told him that I didn't drink he said, "Let's have a smoke then."

So, we sat and smoked his good quality weed.

Brian told me he had set up the original Cafe Freedom in Phnom Pehn a well-known bar right at the heart of darkness. It was a shady area, to say the least, where guns were often displayed by the not-so-subtle local gangsters. We chatted for hours reminiscing our past. Brian's wife served us coffee and snacks whilst his son ran around the yard playing with the dog.

Brian told me if I wanted to set up a place like his, it would cost me around £4000 but that investment would last a lifetime. Then going on to say, "You won't make money but you can live well."

Replying said "Let me give it some thought,"

I told Brian, "I have to go now but will catch up later when I return from Thailand."

We exchanged telephone numbers and shook hands. I enjoyed his company and his down-to-earth attitude but he was still a little on the wild side for the supposedly new reformed me.

Upon getting back to the guesthouse, I lay down thinking what Brian had told me about setting up a place, but that thought soon was out of my mind. My plans were more about setting up a school and teaching English. I still had this unsettling feeling reoccurring since my arrival in this country. It had the taste of urgency and occasional flashes popped into my head of that drug-induced night at the gang hut in Glasgow. It was something continually tugging at my spirit trying to merge and fuse me with something still unknown. I mostly ignored it. I had a distinct sense that the child's spirit always made her presence when she was around evil, or in decadent surroundings. My mind didn't want to go down that road into the spiritual abyss. It seemed as clear as day this spirit was telling me something - had I fallen under her spell or was I possibly cursed?

SEX TEXT AND ATM

Don had said he would meet me at the Stereo bar on Eckerech Street in Thailand. I wanted to be rid of the burden of responsibility for his eight thousand dollars' cash plus the stones and gold that I had secured around my neck in a passport holder. I had only arrived at the hotel bar a short time before Don made his entrance and shook my hand.

Don immediately handed me a Thai sim card saying, "Put that into your phone so we can keep in touch whilst you are here."

I checked in saying hello to the owner and his Thai wife then went upstairs to my room.

I was one floor above where Don slept so dropped my bag and then returned down to his room. I handed over the money and jewellery glad to have it out of my hands.

Don peeled off 10 x $100 bills and handed them to me saying, "Have a holiday, enjoy yourself. You are not at a monastery now."

I felt tired after the trip, which had taken several hours from the border. I thanked my friend for the money then returned to my room to shower and rest.

Don wasn't the type of guy to beat around the bush. What you saw is what you got, there wasn't any pretence. As the saying goes, he 'shot from the hip'. He had good dress sense, fashionable and immaculate. He enjoyed good food wine, and a wide variety of company. Don's associates ranged from criminals to businessmen and especially good-looking women.

Don knocked on my room after midnight standing there with a stunning-looking Thai woman with a short skirt, and long legs. Don introduced her to me this is Nok. I nodded my head and said, "Hello."

She had an air of self-confidence about her.

They both sat on the bed while I rubbed the sleep from my eyes. For some unknown reason, Nok immediately started telling me that she had contact with spirits. Nok continued that we should go to the temple to see what they wanted. I asked Don what was going on with Nok and spirits.

Don nonchalantly replied she was always going to the temple and talking with them. My immediate reaction was one of surprise. I had only met her for five minutes and she was talking about spirits. It got me thinking that maybe the little girl was imposing her supernatural powers on Nok.

Nok told me she was going to introduce me to someone. I didn't need to ask why knowing from past experiences that she thought I would hopefully be a customer for her friend. I washed my face brushed my teeth and dressed in a t-shirt and shorts. Don looked more like the gentleman with long pants and a nice, patterned shirt.

We walked along the main street which was a steady flow of people from all around the world, the night weather was excellent, warm but not too hot. We went into the bar Nok had taken us to and the girl she introduced to me was lovely, she was known as Lek. I smiled at her and she touched my hand.

Lek was small in stature and her tight-fitting attire showed she had the body of a gymnast small-breasted confident smile and all jumpy like she wanted to dance.

Nok was taking care of Don like he was King Solomon and he happily enwrapped himself in the pleasures and affections to be experienced in this exotic land of smiles. The music was loud you could hear the clinking of glasses along with the laughter of these girls sharing their time with foreign men who embraced it wholeheartedly. I excused myself after a couple of hours telling Don my head wasn't up for it tonight and departed.

Lek looked a little disappointed.

The following day as previously planned we were going to see Josh from Chicago at the Cop Shop - a bar in the Jomson area of Pattaya. I knocked on Don's door around midday Nok answered with a towel wrapped around her and a smile that revealed contentment. Don lay on the bed covered with a towel having just come out of the shower.

I took a seat on a chair next to the bed. Don patted his stomach smiling and said this good life is making me fat.

Nok made us all a cup of Ginseng coffee, which Don swore was reducing his weight. I could sense gaining extra pounds bothered his vanity. Don always dressed smartly - it was part of his appeal. I assumed he thought his weight might make him less attractive to women. Although I knew that size wasn't an issue for the women it was how much money they got paid. If he was losing weight, it was more to his sexual activities and not Ginseng coffee.

We left Nok in the room and headed out to his friend's bar.

Don told me a story of how he was keeping three of these ladies on the go at the same time. He showed me his phone that revealed one texted him saying *I love you*, then another had sent him sex messages, and the third always asking for money.

I thought a moment and then said that's about right, sex text and ATM, welcome to the world of tourist prostitution - and the hard-luck stories that go with it.

Don was certainly a sex addict it didn't bother me as he was only interested in mature women. The only negative side if you could call it that was, that he only pursued prostitutes who frequented the red-light district bars with the intention of making money. Don certainly was always a welcome customer he often bought drinks for the women. Don didn't escort them all but he was a generous client to the bar workers. I had already come to terms with this arrangement years ago as long as it was consensual for both parties. My neck was getting painful by turning around and looking at those Thai women on the street that he kept pointing out to me en route to the Cop shop. I couldn't agree with him more they were sexy and the short skirts were tightly fitted on silky soft-skinned legs. I was having all kinds of erotic sex in my mind but still a cold fish when it came to action.

We arrived at the Cop Shop and met the owner who shook my hand and said in a pronounced American accent, "How are you doing brother?"

Don was speaking to me from the side of his mouth and told me that Josh knew a lot of people and some cops from Glasgow came to his place for a drink. Don whispered in my ear that he had slept with a few of the girls the last time he visited. The ladies who worked at the Cop Shop certainly looked inviting.

The conversation led to Don possibly buying over the place next door which was a Gay club but seemingly business wasn't good. We were then joined by two other guys in their 50s from Manchester. I drank water, as they swallowed beer being teetotal can be a wonderful eye-opener when listening to the stories from these guys. The more beers that went down the better the stories became.

It ranged from football rivalry, then eventually to gangster tales, bent cops, and not forgetting bad past wives.

DIARY OF A SAFFRON ASSASSIN

It reminded me of a time long past when travelling in India and had allowed myself the luxury of letting a palm reader get my hand. The way he told me what was going to happen in my future was all too good to be true. The palm reader had told me that I would live a long life. Then went on to say I would come into an unexpected fortune and would meet the woman of my dreams. It was just like these stories I was hearing now. It began to sound like these guys must have met the same palm reader because all their futures were bright - if you believed their stories.

I sat with those guys until evening. We had all eaten Hamburgers with French fries at the Jail Bait Lounge. It was an appropriate name for a bunch of ex-criminals to hang around and to excuse the pun, I bailed myself out. I nodded my head to Don indicating that I was heading back and told him I was going for a nap. Before exiting the place, Josh offered one of the ladies to *arrest me* he handed me a copy of the services available – ranging from ladyboys 'extracting your deepest desire' in the interrogation room to being 'handcuffed and roughed up' but I declined, shook hands all around, and then departed.

The cop shop menu was rather intriguing it made me think about the diversity of sexual pleasures people pursue.

It ranged from heterosexual to homosexual, bondage, and humiliation. I could understand some of the roleplay scenarios. I definitely wouldn't be interested in any interrogation tactics with ladyboys or being handcuffed or ruffed up by them. I had experienced this procedure before but it was not sexually orientated it was while in prison detention in China. I could partly relate with being arrested by a policewoman with a short skirt asking me questions about what I would like to do to her if we were locked in a cell together. I could join the fantasy of laying by a swimming pool with a sexy woman her legs open and straddled on my face dropping unseeded olives into my mouth like I was a Prince in Arabia. As to the other services available it wasn't my cup of tea.

UNPLANNED ENCOUNTER

I was woken at 1:30 pm by a phone call from Nok who was downstairs with Don and wanted me to go out with them. I took a quick shower and then put on clean clothes. I didn't want to go out bar hopping, as the novelty had quickly worn off, but didn't want to offend Don by not going. It was not like the past when I would happily do the bar girl rounds.

I still had the feeling inside me, when watching young women bending in erotic positions. I had my eyes glued seeing them doing a poll dance. These women trying to entice me and others into that jade garden where men of all nations had fought and died for and still do.

The wonderful thing about Pattaya was it never slept.

I eventually left at sunrise walking towards the hotel alone again. On my way there I literally bumped into a drunken lady dressed as if she had come from a birthday party, she still had a paper hat on her head. I got hold of her arm and steadied her.

"Sorry mister," she said.

I asked where are you going and in the same breath said do you want to come to my hotel? She looked at me and answered, "Okay mister," so off we went my heart pounding like a big bass drum.

As we walked towards my hotel, I felt nervous this would be my first intimate encounter with a woman since coming out of prison in China. Whilst I had been at the cop shop my fantasies had been ignited, but fantasy and reality were two different emotions, and at present this was reality. Once we got inside the hotel room she sat down and I asked her name, she told me it was Dai and she was from Laos. Sitting on the bed beside her as she undressed, looking into her eyes I knew nothing would happen as she was too drunk. I felt relieved getting a lucky break and being able to lay beside this woman while she slept – knowing I was looking after her and not abusing her situation. She fell asleep immediately and I gently stroked her face and hair.

I woke up around midday and wanted to do some shopping so left Dai sleeping, upon my return she was sitting on the bed watching television. I wondered if she remembered me.

She smiled saying, "Mr, you are a nice man, you take care of me."

Dai had showered and sat with a towel wrapped over her. She smiled at me again and said, "You take a shower mister."

I stood under the cool water and soaped my body scrubbing all the right places. I didn't have a body spray but felt refreshed. I wrapped the towel around my waist and joined Dai on the bed, Dai placed her head on my shoulder and I put my arm around her waist. It was a safe encounter she had condoms in her bag. I caressed her soft skin it was such a good feeling to climb over the fear of being touched on a physical level. Taking another shower this time together smiling outwardly letting the water fall over me. My mind felt confused and was thinking should I marry this woman she was nice.

Dai went home, and I arranged to meet her again at the hotel later that evening handing her some money and saying this is to pay for your taxi - trying not to offend her by suggesting I was paying for the sex. I then thought again, she is a bar girl wake up.

The over-imaginative thoughts and euphoria of having sex soon wore off coming back to earth again, it is strange how your mind sometimes bends reality.

The fact was she was a working lady who had staggered out drunk from a go-go bar without any customers. Here was me painting a romantic picture in my head having just met this woman and imagined her to be my future wife. All those years of incarceration and loneliness can certainly distort your mind.

Don was surprised that evening when opening his door, he saw me with a woman on my arm. Don then introduced Dai to Nok and the two women immediately began chatting excitedly. Don was giving Dai the eye over then turned to me and said, "She's nice where did you meet her?"

I told him the story, and he smiled saying, "Fate and timing."

Don went on to tell me that Nok had gotten a message about me from the temple spirits - that there would be many deaths near me.

"What does that mean?" I asked.

He replied, "I don't know, why don't you ask her."

She was in conversation with Dai so I thought I would broach the subject later.

We went to visit Walking Street that evening in downtown Pattaya to eat fresh seafood at a restaurant there. I was singing Frankie Miller's song in my head and kept repeating the line *'Drunken nights in the city are taking its toll down were the Buffalo Roam'*. I was feeling perked up and had a spring in my step. I kept smiling at the multitude of foreign travellers who passed along on this same route, and at this moment in time, life felt good.

Nok had ordered wine for her and Dai and a mango shake for me, Don had a beer. It was a lovely location sitting with lights throwing a variety of colours reflecting from the water garden.

I took the opportunity to ask Nok about her visit to the temple. She told me that the temple spirits had told her about a child and a Monk who would kill many people. I asked what has that to do with me? Nok said she did not know but her intuition was there is a girl's spirit who is very troubled.

We left the conversation at that.

Dai and I spent the night with very little conversation, her English was limited to bar talk.

I was looking for a relationship and knew women in this sex trade either by economic difficulties or by force would respect the opportunity to have a chance for something better in life. I was looking for someone similar to myself blemished by past encounters with life, but ready to work for the good of myself and others without greed. Dai had told me she worked at Bobby's bar and she would have to pay a bar fine which was paid by the customer. I didn't mind and having knowledge about the fine from many visits to bars in the past. The usual payment depending on the bar was 300 Thai Bhat for every night the woman didn't go to work. Then upon return to the bar she would pay the owner 300 for each night she wasn't present. I did ask her what I should pay her for staying with me. It is up to you she replied and we left it at that, just enjoying the moment.

We had been in Pattaya for three days when Don phoned me and asked if I was busy, and if could I come down to his room. I just got inside his door when he started cursing that the owner of the hotel was a cheap skate. Don was furious saying he wouldn't even give Nok a bedsheet when she asked for one. "I'm checking out and that bum is not getting paid." He had already packed his bags and said to Nok lets go, I followed him down to the reception.

Don called the owner and immediately started to complain. The guy was trying to explain his case but Don wasn't having any of it. Don said, "When I was going out last night you were sitting with a bottle of Johnny Walker's whiskey drinking and watching television."

"Aye, that's correct the owner replied in his Ayrshire accent saying it was a cup final game and some of the lads got together to watch it."

That was it for Don. "Oh! You charge top rates so you and your pals can watch football, but not get off your ass to fetch a bedsheet for a paying customer."

"Listen," the guy said softly, "there's no need for trouble …"

"Trouble, fucking trouble," Don repeated and grabbed him by the hair and head-butted him on the nose.

The guy collapsed to the floor screaming.

I pulled Don away and he left with Nok but never paid the bill. I said to the guy, "I am moving also."

He sneered back at me and said, "Are you not going to pay your bill either?"

Without replying I went upstairs and packed and was down again in five minutes. I paid my bill and left. It was then I decided my holiday was over and I should make my way back to Cambodia.

I then phoned Don to find out where he was staying, he told me he had moved into the Stereo bar and hotel, just a minute's walk away at the corner of the same street. I checked in there also, Don assured me this was a better place as he had stayed here before, but it had had no rooms this time when he'd initially returned. I stayed a couple more days taking Dai shopping and buying her nice little bits and pieces of clothing, and we always ate well.

It was my last night so the four of us returned to the walking street and ate good seafood again. I hadn't given any illusion to

Dai that I would be returning. The last night in Pattaya was light and fun and I even took a glass of wine. It felt strange putting alcohol into my body after so many years. I was in a good mood and felt like celebrating having overcome my fear of being intimate with a woman again. Having spent a total of five nights with Dai and of course, we did have some day outings and lots of fun. In the morning we ate breakfast across from the hotel that was where the minibus was picking me up. I looked at her while she ate, she was nice and I was thankful to have met her. Dai didn't speak much English and that had gotten tiring in the short time knowing her. I appreciated having that warm loving touch of a woman, someone, to snuggle up to and cuddle. It was a good feeling and it recharged my soul, a healing had occurred within me making me feel that I was now approachable.

LIFE TIME VISA

I had heard about this visa you could acquire for one hundred American dollars which lasted for life. It could be given at the border crossing from Thailand. It also had the benefit of not having to leave the country to renew it.

I made inquiries from the guy at the immigration desk regarding this visa and he directed me to go into the office next door. Upon entering the room, a group of officials sat around smoking and drinking tea. One of them waved me over and pointed to a seat then he took a form from his desk and handed it to me. I didn't have to fill out the form but had to sign the one he gave me. It was a simple exchange of $100 and got myself that special visa stamped into my passport.

That visa allowed me to register and open a business under the relevant Cambodian laws. In my mind, this country was giving opportunities to people to invest and also help rebuild their economy, infrastructure, and tourist industry, which was beginning to boom. It was a good deal knowing that I didn't have to travel to the border every month to renew my visa. It was better still knowing I could work here and be useful as an English teacher. It had been part of the reason for coming here to assist with education and could also sustain a basic living standard.

I still had the journey with the boat to go and was feeling tired. The trip back to Sihanoukville was uneventful and would be glad to be at the villa again to lay my bag down and take a long slow shower, put on the kettle for coffee, and smoke a joint.

Living at the Villa was something special for me just the size of the place having three bedrooms and an outside porch to lay on my hammock. I was never without food, as the local food was cheap and tasty.

My main priority was the quality of life and how to integrate with my surroundings. My savings allowed me a limited budget I could live for a couple of years before my money ran out. That was if I didn't take up any more vices other than smoking marijuana. I had experienced my intimate encounter in Thailand and it was certainly in my mind to do it again. I did notice a change in my thinking after the Conrad incident. My mind couldn't fully focus. I seemed to be always torn between my first intention of coming here then being influenced by the spirit girl. I had $600 each month to get me by and was trying to live like a native as much as a foreigner could.

I began visiting a Buddhist Temple a few times each week where the orphan children lived and gave a few English classes to some of the monks and children there. I wanted to be occupied and teaching was something that I could do. I also had been frequenting Chamois Frog Shack which was a very popular place to meet up with other foreigners. It put a strain on my budget by buying seafood and marijuana shakes. I decided to buy myself a cheap camera to start taking photos of what I wanted to portray on my canvases. It was the poverty mixed with affluence, sex trade, drugs, and religion that seemed to me to be one big abstract canvas.

One day at the beach a woman approached me and asked, "Do you like massage mister? This is my daughter she is very good."

She presented to me a beautiful mixed-race child aged around fourteen. The woman told me the girl's father was German.

I asked where the father was now but she had no history of him to tell me. I guessed he didn't even know he had a child. I guessed he was a tourist and probably just a one-night stand. I sensed this woman was trying to set guys up for a bust to get money from them by having underage sex with her daughter. If it wasn't that she was a fucking bitch for trying to sell her child into prostitution under the guise of a massage.

I was having nothing to do with it and so removed myself immediately from her presence - heart pounding and angry.

I needed funding of some sort if I wanted to contribute to my new homeland. My visit to the beach three or more times a week started to get boring. Although I was getting inspired to paint new canvases, I was also getting fed up with the traffic down there. It was mostly young travellers partying, or mature men laying on deck chairs beside young beauties. On top of that the rows of begging, part limbless, victims of the past horrors under the Pol Pot regime were getting under my skin. The Khmer Rouge inflicted a near genocide on the population with a loss of between one and a half million people and the effects were clear to see even now.

Cambodia was a beautiful place but poverty and corruption were rife. I could visualize Cambodia opening up to Western influence imagining the youth in the not-so-distant future struggling through another type of horror on the Pinocchio long-nosed lying and deceitful consumer trail that would be brought along with the economic benefits attained by Western influence. I could already see nearly every teenager had a mobile phone in their hands and wearing emblazoned T-shirts with celebrity images on them. The traditional attire was now only worn by men and women in their 30s or over.

DIARY OF A SAFFRON ASSASSIN

.oOo.

When I travelled back to Cambodia from Thailand, I sat next to a guy about my age who had a very distinguished aristocratic accent. During the trip, we started chatting, and I told him my reasons for coming to Cambodia. I started by telling him about my intention of staying at a meditation retreat, then eventually going on about me being in jail in China.

He was a bouncing board for me and I wanted to hear his thoughts regarding my past. The feedback from him was positive saying cannabis wasn't a harmful drug, unlike many that were accessible on the streets today. Adam had listened during the long journey and asked me if it would be okay to give my story to his friend Andrew who was an Asian press reporter. I replied let me think about that.

We exchanged email addresses and shook hands. I really did unload onto this poor guy who was probably hoping for a quiet journey to reflect on his own affairs.

It was about one week later when I received an email from Andrew in Bangkok, saying he would be interested in doing a story on me would it be okay? I replied yes and sent him my phone number. I had told Don about what was going on and he replied be careful what you tell these guys as you should well know they often publish lies and scandal. Don was nobody's fool he mistrusted lawyers, police, and the press.

I got a phone call a few days later from Andrew asking where we could meet as he was here in Sihanoukville. I gave him directions to meet me at the top of our road. Andrew looked to be in his early fifties, he had tiredness in his eyes his companion was tall, aged around forty, carrying a camera bag. His name was Peter. After we shook hands and introduced ourselves, we went into the Villa and sat down.

"I see that you paint," Andrew commented.

"Yes, that's correct," I told him going on to say that I was self-taught whilst in jail in China. The interview was direct and straight to the point. Andrew asked questions while Peter took some photos. Andrew wanted to know my reason for being in Cambodia. I told him my intention for leaving Scotland was to go into a Monastery and that living in Glasgow with a depressive outlook was killing me inwardly. He then asked about my time in China. I told him about the prison conditions and other things he wanted to know about me. His associate was taking photos of my paintings while we spoke.

The interview was over and we shook hands. Andrew said he would return tomorrow to take a photo shoot up at the Monastery. We shook hands as they departed and arranged that we could meet up later that evening at Victory Hill in a French restaurant.

Don returned after they had gone and asked me how things went and told him my thoughts that both guys at least seemed genuine. I could see the cynical twist coming onto Don's lip as if to say aye right the press is genuine.

I did respect Don's views and insight regarding being wary of the press. I told Don we were invited to eat that evening and show them around town.

We met up at the allocated place and I introduced Don to the reporters. Most of the conversation was about what was going on around us as we were in the red-light district. It was a sleazy place with little or no sophistication.

"Unlike Thailand," Andrew commented.

We all nodded our heads agreeing on that. Peter, Andrew, and Don were knocking back a couple of beers while I drank water. They ordered wine and the chat was flowing freely.

Andrew said to me take a drink of wine you're on holiday, relax, but I declined.

Both reporters had been working in Asia and had lived half their lives going from one country to another covering stories.

After eating we went into a bar the two reporters never allowed the girls to impose themselves on them but bought some of them a drink. Don had good company that night, these guys wanted to enjoy themselves by having a binge with alcohol but had no intention of any sexual contact. There were a few lewd comments from the women but said more through ignorance and mischief with no malice intended.

Andrew noticed that none of the girls were attending to me and leaned over saying, "Enjoy yourself."

It must have been the saffron suit, shaved head and only drinking water that put them off and that's why I wore it.

The following morning, early, Andrew was at the gate. We jumped onto two motorcycles and took off to the Wat Leu Temple. The weather was warm and the motorbike driver I always took handed me his cap – saying, "Teacher, cover your head." I was teaching him his wife and daughter English and they became my first Cambodian friends.

The drive there was quite scenic in parts riding above the port area onto a small hill we could see the coastline then off the side road to the temple grounds.

Peter took numerous photos and we spoke with some of the monks and children. Andrew commented on the state of their decayed teeth.

I replied to him immediately, saying, "Dental hygiene that's what I will teach them next lesson."

We returned from the photo shoot and planned to meet up with them again later at Chaimoi Frog Shack at the beach.

Lying under the fan in my bedroom back at the Villa after the photo shoot my mind was seeing images of the children's gums at the temple.

At the forefront was the image of that little girl from the killing fields encounter, she was looking at me, trying to tell me something. Then my thoughts replayed stories in my head that Andrew had told me he had covered. The stories ranged from chopped-up bodies in Thailand, done by desperate criminals. Then other brutal assaults were inflicted on foreigners who had abused someone's sister. Most of the stories were horrific outright intimidation to make the foreigner leave Thailand, so as to take over their business or property. Andrew had eventually gone on to the paedophile case of a well-known British pop star whom he had written about.

I got out of bed a few hours later, not feeling refreshed, still muddled in my mind, reminiscing the horror tales from Andrew. I then got dressed and headed out to the beach. Andrew greeted me with a handshake we sat on the bamboo chairs facing the water.

Peter hadn't arrived yet, there were a couple of other travellers close by smoking and taking in the sunset. Peter arrived ten minutes later and bought two beers and a fruit shake for me; he had hardly got his ass on the chair before he proceeded to tell me his thoughts.

Peter said, "You're the Saffron Assassin."

I looked at him, replying, "That is a rather abstract statement. What makes you think that?"

Andrew laughed at this comment and said, "Your past life of drug smuggling plus your life in Scotland was often violent, and here you are now dressed in saffron studying to become a monk."

I didn't pursue this comment any further but it had turned on a light in my mind. I was immediately transported back to the

Gang Hut in Glasgow and the echo of a voice saying you should go and murder that Pop Star paedophile in Vietnam.

Andrew brought me back to the moment saying, "Come on pal, wake up."

It took me out of my daydream.

GUNS, DOGS, AND RUSSIANS

Since arriving back at the Villa, Don had taken another trip to Thailand. I had noticed that someone moved into the house next door having seen the jeep parked in the yard. I continued getting myself settled back in giving the new neighbour no further thought. Then in the middle of the night, I was awakened by a dog barking but went back to sleep.

Don arrived a few days later with Noi it was early evening. The following morning Don asked me did you hear those dogs barking last night?

"Yes," I replied, "and I have heard them every day and night since coming back from Pattaya."

Don was livid, he couldn't believe it. He went on to tell me they were howling for hours. As the nights went on the dogs' barking began to wake me, but I continued to ignore them. I was trying to explain my theory about zoning out the dogs barking one morning after Don had another sleepless night. I went on to explain to him it depends if something gets into your psyche and begins to irritate your nerves.

I gave him the example of a dripping water tap. I said when you get attached to that sound then you're fucked. I could see my theory had gone it one ear and out the other. Don wasn't listening. He turned his eyes up and gave me a wry grin and ended up staying at a hotel in town so he could get some sleep. The following day Don escorted Noi to the terminal as she was going back home a little fatter (not in her stomach, but in her pocket). Don was certainly a kind man with money.

It wasn't long before the dog barking got to me too, the early morning daybreak was pierced by a caged dog howl instead of the songbirds.

Don called a meeting with the Villa owner and asked him to sort out the dog problem and he said he would, but one week later it was still the same. Don called another meeting with the owner and it was decided to put up a corrugated fence on the gate so the dogs wouldn't be disturbed by any passers-by. The fence was put up and nothing changed they still howled all night and most of the day.

Som from Angkor real estate was the one who signed the contract for them to move into the house next door. Don asked him how long they would stay. Their boss had signed a six-month contract Som replied, which meant twenty more weeks of sleepless nights.

It had gotten to the point that Don was threatening to go next door with the automatic pistol that he had purchased from a bent cop and shoot the fucking dog.

Don had tried again and again to solve the dog issue. Now he was going to take the matter into his own hands.

I told him to hold on, "Don why don't we just put a sleeping tablet into a piece of meat and throw it down into the yard tonight."

Don said, "Okay, let's do that." Then he went on to tell me the guy's next door were Vietnamese and were working on a building site for the Russians. Don raved on about why they didn't keep their dogs outside the fucking Russian's house? "I will tell you why," he went on, "because the fucking Russians would just shoot the dog that is why."

That evening after Don threw a couple of lumps of cooked meat with crushed Valium inside, we never heard a sound from the dogs again. The reason for that was they didn't wake up.

I asked, "How many sedatives did you put into that meatball?"
Don smiled and told me, "Ten."
"That's enough to kill a fucking horse," I told him.
He just laughed in response.
The feedback we heard from other neighbours was all good, it certainly stopped the noise. Don sometimes gets things done his own way, regardless of the consequences, and in this case, there were none.

HEADLINE NEWS

In Sihanoukville, there had been a small explosion of internet shops opening. It was expanding everywhere, and everyone was looking to make money. I was not that computer savvy but I did know how to do a Google search and to write and save a document.

One day Don asked me to send an email on his behalf to a holistic retreat that was offering a variety of healing treatments. We returned to the internet shop the following day to check if there was any response.

I got an email that day from my friend Paul from Glasgow along with a photo with the newspaper heading. I asked the guy at the café to print it out for me. Paul sent the article in the Mail on Sunday it came with a photo of me walking with two monks outside the monastery. Paul said that he and his brother who owned hydroponic shops in Glasgow would help me to set up some educational programs. I presented the printed-out email to Don who was laughing at the newspaper headline. We both laughed together at the choice of words '*Ex Gangster in Cambodia*'.

Don let out a war cry, "Tongs Ya Bass!" which was the gang's name that we ran about with in the 1960s. Don and I sat and read the article whilst having a coffee. The headline used the terminology Ex- Gangster Don and I joked about this. When we were growing up a Gangster in our young minds was Al Capone in the American Mafia in Glasgow we were referred to as thugs or hooligans.

As we got up to leave Don commented that's quite a positive article but started laughing again saying, "Fucking press like to catch readers attention with spectacular headlines."

Don had received a reply from the holistic treatment centre with an attachment and asked me to open it. It had details of the location and prices on it. Don asked me if we could keep the file.

I said, "It will always be there in the inbox, you can read it anytime." I explained to him that we could have it printed now, then went back to the counter and asked the guy if he could help me to print the attachment.

Don told me about a German guy who rented a shop on the main road into town but close to our Villa and said the guy was leaving and maybe I should talk with him about renting it.

I went over to the shop Don had mentioned the following morning and introduced myself to Roland who was about my age. I asked him for more details about renting the shop. Roland told me the rent was $200 each month plus paying electric and water as separate bills.

He went on to say, "If you want to move in now, I have paid one-year rent in advance that expires in January." Roland wanted to leave and that was obvious, so we worked on a deal.

It was now the end of April which meant eight-month rent equalled $1600 plus he wanted me to pay for the fittings another $600. Roland was trying to put a value on the location but I wasn't having that, saying look around you this area is not exactly in the town. We agreed on a deal and I ended up paying him $1800 all in - that included a two-bedroom house with shop-attached furniture and cable television. I had all the legal paperwork done within one week and signed a new contract in my name for a five-year lease.

I had the good intention of opening a tea shop where young people could come and learn to sketch still-life objects. On top of that idea, they could practice to read, write and speak English. I hadn't given it much forethought my idea was to have signs on the walls in basic English. I intended to put paper and pencils on the tables and pamphlets with greetings such as good morning, afternoon, and evening. It would be a trial-and-error attempt to do something useful and positive I had spoken with an American lady who ran the Starfish bakery in town about opening an art and English School and her advice was not to open a school but to go and help at one. I considered her good advice that doing a job hands-on at an already established school could be more rewarding than setting something new up. I got in touch with Kon who worked at Angkor's real estate agency. I asked if he knew of any school that I could teach at. Kon took me to a place where railway children lived in dilapidated carriages. It was unhygienic, to say the least. The place was awful and they had a rust-laden and splintered wooden hovel to study in. After taking some photos I sent them to Paul plus an estimate on how much it would cost to run and improve the conditions. My friend Paul knew how to build websites and if I wanted to promote and advertise my plan to assist with education in Cambodia. I needed his expert assistance.

It would need a certain amount of money per year to employ another teacher plus for renovations. I had also sent Paul photos of the surroundings and within one week he emailed me saying he had built a website. I opened up the website and there were my photos, plus a letter asking for donations to run and renovate the dilapidated old train carriages. I took Don to the internet shop later that afternoon and showed him the website, he was delighted and also fascinated by how quickly things could get done by email. It was a pleasant surprise when Don contributed $500 to the renovation project. Thanks to Don, the two guys from the press, and the Hemphouse crew for placing a soothing footprint onto aching soil in Cambodia.

ENTRAPMENT

I had watched a program on television about undercover police tracking a paedophile ring. Those underage girls were being groomed to perform live sexual acts with much older men on video. In that program, the police went to raid the house of the perpetrators but when they arrived the house was already cleared out. It was obvious someone had informed the paedophile ring organisers beforehand. The indication from the documentary could only be someone in the police force had passed on the word exposing their intended raid operation.

It was a wet morning; the rain was battering against the bedroom window but I decided to go into town to Ana's internet to check my email.

I was pleased to receive two emails, one from my American friend Hank who was currently in China he had been studying Buddhism and living in temples for over two decades practicing Vipassana meditation. The other was from Andrew the news reporter and he asked me to meet a friend of his at a bar called the Sweetheart Bar in Phnom Penh. He sent his associate's name and phone number saying that all my expenses would be covered and a bit more on top. Andrew explained that his associate was on the trial of a serial sex offender. This friend of his was going to catch and expose him but needed help he explained to me that it was a local policeman he is after and not a foreigner. I reread the email and then wrote down the phone number plus the meeting place address.

I went back to the Villa to visit Don, telling him about the email he listened and said, "What the fuck are these guys up to asking to you get involved in that sort of shit?" Don went on saying, "Stay away from those cunts!"

I had already made up my mind, that I was going. Fate and timing seemed very relevant again at this moment. I could taste the fear along with excitement rising inside me, along with that not-so-innocent scent from the spirit girl who was now permanently present but whom I tried mostly to ignore.

I arrived in Phnom Penh, checked into the Hope and Anchor guesthouse, dropped my bag, took a shower then lay naked on the bed still wet - the fan on full to cool me down. I had been having this reoccurring dream of the little girl's skull after the monastery encounter, the sad-eyed smile had gone from her face and was now more like a sneering grin.

I left the guesthouse around sunset, sitting down and watching the skyline, it was magnificent. I was drinking good coffee at the Woolly Rhino bar on the lakeside. The sun had already set and the cloud formation was pushing down on me in an odd sort of way. It hadn't been my decision nor idea that Phnom Penh would be my spy ground on a paedophile hunt. I had dressed mostly in saffron attire since my arrival in Cambodia and had gained a little respect from the local people for my monk lifestyle. The street had now become a constant beeping of horns and not a place to be between 5am and 7am - it was pandemonium. The air was polluted, stealing the earlier tranquillity of the sunset.

I had phoned Gavin whilst at the coffee shop, and he arrived shortly after my call. He was from New Zealand, in his early thirties and had black hair tied in a ponytail.

I sat and listened to his plan, it was about a local policeman who had been sexually abusing girls and forcefully putting them into brothels. Gavin went on to tell me he had followed this guy and located his house. I inquired, so how can I assist you? Gavin explained he had followed this guy to a certain brothel on more than one occasion and wanted to catch him in the act taking a girl inside. It was his plan for me to go into that brothel and ask for a girl under the age of twelve.

I looked at him and thought this guy must be off his bloody tree. I then I wondered if I was being set up to be framed and arrested?

Don had said to me before I left to be wary of the press, "They don't only look for the scandals, they create them."

I asked Gavin, "What is the use in me going to ask for paedophile sex?" stuttering these words out and being stirred in the throes of another emotional choking storm.

Gavin went on to explain that if I made that request for the young girl the mamasan of the brothel would contact this policeman and he would fulfil her request at a price.

"What is the fucking use of that?" I was raising my voice and felt like I was losing my mind? I sneered at him saying, "You get photos of a corrupt cop and a child gets kidnapped? Fuck off!" I spat.

The sudden movement of me getting from my chair to leave surprised Gavin and he said, "Sit down, please. He isn't going to get away with her."

Gavin went on to explain he had set up motorbike watchers from a Non-Government Organization that worked with abused children and the policeman would be apprehended as soon as he lifted a child from the street.

I listened to this part of the story and it made more sense to catch him red-handed whether it was entrapment or not.

Gavin laid out the approach I was to take. I was to go into the brothel and simply ask for a girl under twelve. Gavin had told me not to bargain with the price and to demand the girl be available on that day or evening.

We sat and discussed more details he then handed me $300. I got onto his motorbike and we stopped outside the brothel I was to go to. I took a mental note of the location and we left. After returning to my hotel, I sat with my chest pounding and afraid of being set-up, walking into a paedophile's den. The paranoia was leaping from me, while the sensation of the little girl's hand tingled adrenalin up and down my spine. She was keeping me attached to revenging the death cries of the abused. The invasion of my psyche at the killing fields was real and present but I was still in denial.

The following morning, I got out of bed at 5. am I stood in front of the mirror, eyeballing myself and staring until a vision of the child appeared. I watched as her child's hand reached up and held onto mine. I could feel her little fist around my finger.

The reflection in the mirror was clear, but when I turned to acknowledge her, she was gone.

I went back into the bedroom and sat in the lotus position on the floor, meditating until hours later when the sun was well up. Then I took a shower, dressed in smart pants, and a clean shirt, putting a hat on to partly shade my features.

I had rehearsed the procedure over and over again imagining myself walking into a brothel my eyes down and asking for something that disgusted me whilst opening my wallet and flashing $100 bills.

I did several re-runs, looked into the mirror, checked out my acting skills, and then went downstairs to eat breakfast. I called Gavin to let him know I was on my way to the designated brothel. I left the hotel and proceeded to my assignment, feeling my heart rate had calmed considerably and felt I was doing something worthy for the community in this land of horrors.

I finally arrived at the brothel taking a slow deep breath through my nostrils and walked straight inside. I was met with the sight of young pyjama-clad girls, at a glance they looked all under sixteen.

"Welcome Sir," a woman in her forties smiled at me. "What do you like sir?" She took my arm and turned me around to view the girls.

"Do you have a virgin?" I asked.

"Yes, sir," she replied.

"I want a virgin, but she must be young."

"No problem, sir how old do you like sir?"

I said, "Twelve years old or under, and I want her today."

"Sir," she said, "tonight ok sir. You come back at ten o'clock sir, but you give me money now."

I hadn't stuck to my script and asked how much. $200 sir."

I handed her a $100 bill saying I would pay the rest when I met the girl. I got out of that place fast, but not too fast, as to bring suspicion on myself. I then phoned Gavin to meet me. We met back at the Sweetheart bar and I gave him the rundown of my events. A satisfied smile spread across his face as he got onto his mobile phone and put his plan into action.

I said, "Good luck," and asked him to phone me about the outcome as I was leaving for Sihanoukville the following day.

I was asleep when my mobile phone rang, it was Gavin telling me that the guy had slipped their loop and had delivered the girl to the brothel. I sat up and said, "What did you just say?"

He then repeated himself.

I shouted through the phone, "You fucking scumbag, get in there and get her out."

"I can't," he replied, "but you can."

"What are you talking about?"

He reminded me that the girl was for me. I didn't know what the time was until looking at the mobile it was just after 9 pm and I had only slept a couple of hours.

"I am on my way and will call you back." I got dressed in minutes and ran out the door. The hot night air was suffocating and my overbeating heart caused the sweat beads to run down my face and back in a panic attack. I dialled Gavin's number as I walked.

"I don't think you can do anything," he informed me over the phone, "just go there and pay the money to sit with her in the room."

I shouted over the phone, "What do you mean to *sit with her*? You're telling me not to take her out of there because your shit-filled idea and trap has involved me in a kidnapping and child abuse. I am going to kill your bastard face." I shouted through the phone and hung up. I stopped a taxi and then got off near the location. I walked fast and was now drawing attention to myself in the haste of reaching that girl on time before some sicko got there before me.

I tried to slow my heart rate but it was on overdrive as I walked into the brothel. The same girls sat around like pockmarked porcelain dolls. The Mama-San was soon on the scene took my arm and led me behind a curtain and down a narrow hallway into a room. A young girl sat there red-eyed but amazingly calm, she never looked up. I had the impulse to snatch her and take off but chose to use the old custom of bartering.

I asked again, "How much do I have to pay?"

"$100 Sir, short time Sir. She virgin Sir - no need a long-time Sir."

I then asked her how much for the whole night $300 Sir."

I thought this was a cheap exchange for saving a child. I agreed and paid her another $200 and made the move to collect the girl.

"Sorry, Sir, no-can-do Sir, her too young. You have a problem at the hotel, Sir."

I impulsively replied, "I have my own house."

I saw her eyes light up and she said, $350 Sir, but bring her back tomorrow ok sir? Where is your house Sir?" she asked.

I put my finger to my lips indicating no comment and gave my full Mandarin smile, then paid her the final instalment.

I left thinking I had done a good deed in my life and was surprised the little girl didn't seem unsettled taking my hand as we departed. I hadn't given any thought about how it would appear with me walking down the street at this time of night with a little girl by my side. I phoned Gavin and he picked me up took the girl and said he would contact me tomorrow. I walked into the night and felt that distinct tug at my soul telling me my mission had not been completed. In the forefront of my mind, the spirit girl reminded me not to forget that the corrupt scumbag policeman was still out there.

The following morning Gavin called and told me he took the girl to his house last night and was taking her to a shelter later to locate her family. I asked why not ask the little girl to take you to her house? Gavin told me that there were office procedures that had to be carried out and that she was sleeping at the moment still traumatized. I asked Gavin if he could take me to the house where that scumbag policeman lived. I made it clear to him that I wanted to see if this guy was for real after the stress and paranoia, I had endured the night before and he agreed to pick me up.

It was a couple of hours later Gavin joined me outside my hotel and I jumped onto the back of his motorbike it was only a ten-minute journey and he stopped outside at a corner shop selling noodles. We ordered some food and he pointed out the house to me. It had a high decorative iron fence around it and a drive-in gate that lay open. I looked at the place seeing that this guy lived well for someone on a normal policeman's salary with a fancy gated property.

I saw a silhouette of the little spirit girl in one of the windows beckoning to me go inside - she was reminding me that this was not over yet.

Gavin spoke taking me away from my muse, saying, "Let's go." Letting me know that he had work to do and thanked me for the risk I had taken. Gavin apologised for the fuck up the night before and then reimbursed me for my services.

I got onto the back of his motorbike and he dropped me off outside my guest house. Before leaving Gavin assured me that he would get that bastard soon. We had arranged to meet again that evening for dinner.

As I sat there in my room thinking what could or should be done about this fuckwit abuser and a plan of action came to mind involving putting on my robes again. That evening during dinner Gavin had told me that he suspected the police officer knew that his office was onto him. He then went on to say he must have a network protecting him. Gavin's eyes narrowed as a look of determination crossed his face. "I can't let him get away with it," he said. "I have to take matters into my own hands.

I swallowed hard, nodding my head in understanding.

It was an intense conversation and I wished Gavin luck in eventually catching the abuser. I had other plans in mind which I didn't disclose. The only way I knew of him not escaping justice was to garrotte him the same way I had done to Conrad.

I couldn't help but feel the weight of the girl's spirit and the responsibility resting on my shoulders. My mind had been filled with visions of terrible crimes committed against innocent children. I knew I had to do something.

DIARY OF A SAFFRON ASSASSIN

I got out of bed at 4:30 am put on my robe then made my way to the abuser's house. I approached the premises cautiously as I walked through the iron gate onto the path, I was thinking again about how he could afford such a property on his merger salary. I stood there for a minute frustration etched across my face. I then climbed through an open window and quietly tiptoed inside the house. I saw his police uniform jacket hanging in the hallway. I was looking for any indication if he was married such as children's toys or women's clothing but didn't see anything. I then entered his bedroom, ready to expose the heinous crimes and bring justice to the innocent children who had suffered under his dark reign.

I threw a few sheets of paper onto the floor which I had prepared whilst writing my mantra. I gave details of his crimes which I had been told about from Gavin along with the address of the brothel. I looked at his face resting on two pillows his neck exposed then proceeded to garrotte him. It gave me a thrill feeling his body struggle to be free from my gras. Looking into his bloodshot eyes and his eventual last gasp for air.

I completed my ritual by sticking a mantra up his ass spat on his face and left. As I exited the gate several monks looked at me with surprise in their eyes. I bowed my head as I passed them by.

I returned to the guest house and took a shower whilst the cold water cleansed my body - but my soul still felt unclean. I had enjoyed watching this policeman die. I didn't have that feeling when taking Conrad's life, something had changed inside me. I thought it might have been because I had seen the behaviour firsthand with Conrad but with the policeman, I could only imagine the horror he had inflicted on children. As I dried myself my spirit companion looked radiant at my side. I thought back to the newspaper article about me bringing karma to Cambodia's killing fields. I remembered saying to the reporter that I wouldn't kill an ant but I had never said I wouldn't kill human vermin.

BACK IN SIHANOUKVILLE

I arrived back in Sihanoukville feeling somewhat elated but also a haze in my head due to the pleasure I had felt taking the evil policeman's life. I went over to visit Don, and he inquired as to how my trip went? all was good I said but they never caught the culprit. I then went on to say that he hadn't shown face whilst I was there. I never mentioned the whole scenario about me going to the brothel, nor the other part about myself visiting the abuser's house - that would remain my secret.

During his previous stay in Cambodia, which was the year before, Don told me a story that he had been making friends with several of the local beach vendors. Don sometimes offered them to sit with him out of the sun.

It was during one of those very hot days that he had asked a few of the women if they had ever visited Angkor Wat, and they replied that they hadn't. A local ladyboy who hung around with these vendors said they could not afford to go but would like to, someday. Don being over-generous at times replied, "I will take you, when do you want to go?"

After some excited chatter, it was decided they would think about it and let him know the following day.

It was now over eight months later one of the ladies, called Mong, met up with Don and me at the beach, they greeted each other like old friends. Mong ran off to tell the other women that Don had returned. As the days passed these women would join us and eat and drink for free at the expense of my kind-hearted friend. Mong also reminded him of what he had said about visiting Angkor Wat. Don true to his word got them together and this is what unfolded.

Don paid for the first-class bus, plus booked them into a 3-star hotel gave Mong $100 to pay for the entrance fee into Angkor Wat plus gave her $20 to give each of the women as spending money. That amount of money was the equivalent of what they might have earned after a month or more trudging the beach selling low-quality tourist items.

It was a once-in-a-lifetime opportunity, so off the four of them went - all with a smile on their faces.

When they returned from the trip, I got to hear the gossip from Don. The ladyboy had told him that Mong had kept the money for the entrance fee - because local people entering the grounds was free. The other money was to be used for expenses such as food and drinks but she had kept that also. It was clear Mong was making a serious effort at getting my friend to sleep with her after her return from Angkor Wat. I noticed she had begun to dress to impress, although, in a cheap cotton outfit, it was tight fitting and certainly showed her curves.

Don didn't like that trait in people's character and when he next saw her at the beach she came with the usual smile and greetings. Mong then sat down uninvited, which you do take for granted when you think someone is your friend.

Don let her go on about how wonderful it was to visit Angkor Wat, and then he asked her about paying for the entrance and the money he gave her for the other women to which she had no reply.

When he told me about their meeting, I could taste the bitterness of his disappointment for what had happened. It wasn't the right time for me to tell him that the sort of kindness he had shown would not always be appreciated. I knew it could be exploited and it had been in Don's case.

I reminded him there are a lot of desperate and hungry people here and it's not only for money and food and it is not only Khmers. I pointed out the vast foreign influx of all sorts of deviants and perverts, some even fugitives from the law back in their own countries, lived among us. In my past travels around Asia, I was mostly oblivious to what was going on around me mostly due to being high on drugs. I had this awareness that, here in Cambodia, it felt like someone was giving me a true picture of daily life, not seen in tour brochures.

.oOo.

At the beach a while back, I met a young English guy called Tim, he was telling stories about living in Cambodia which he had done for the past few years. One story was of a teenage love infatuation with a young Khmer lady called Tang. Tim had told me she followed him everywhere, but she was young around eighteen and he had befriended her and her family. She was now twenty and Tim was still her main focus. I listened closely to his stories of how she constantly sent texts and phoned him, and as far as Tim was concerned, she did everything but jump on him. Tim knew that touching one of those local girls meant marriage or money, so he hadn't touched her he assured me.

I had been living at the shop now going over a month when Don called in for a cup of tea and a chat. He began telling me about this woman he had met. I was waiting to hear his usual compliment that she had a body to die for but he didn't say it. Don told me her name was Tang and she was on her way to meet him when she had a motorbike crash. "I sent her to the doctor to get a checkup and told her to give the medical bill to me." Don with his compassionate heart was always there to help as if the accident was his doing.

Don explained due to the fact she was on the way to meet him, he felt responsible. It wasn't until more than a week later that I discovered it was the same Tang that English Tim at the beach had been telling me about.

Don came over to visit me asking, "Do you remember that girl I told you about who had the accident?"

"Sure," I said.

"Well, she is moving into my place tomorrow, but she will have her own room." Don made it very clear there was no sex involved. I had my doubts, as you would, judging by his track record.

As the weeks went by Don's attitude changed. Initially, it was, "It's great to have someone to make you coffee and home-cooked food; somebody, to clean the place and do your laundry." But it quickly became "What the hell Loc, she thinks I am a mobile ATM. The medical bill is ongoing, with prescriptions and checkups."

Don then started paying Tang for the cooking and cleaning $50 a month. She had even begun going out at night and not returning he said.

I was getting tired of listening to the stories about missing pots, and other bits and pieces that Tang had taken to her brother's boat. I knew my friend had a soft spot for beautiful sexy women. I couldn't fathom what he was trying to prove if anything. It was the same story over again. Don was complaining about not getting what he wanted out of the relationship if it wasn't sex.

I did go on to say, "You have to find the middle ground, my friend, because giving to the needy beats giving to the greedy."

Don gave it some thought, then said, "You are right pal, I will put an end to it as soon as she comes back."

It had been five days that passed by then with no texts, and no calls.

I replied, "That tells you something, doesn't it? If she hasn't been back for days, you no longer have to care for her. I finished by saying, "Do you know what Tang means in Chinese?"

"No," Don replied.

"It means sugar and this one is thinking you are her sugar daddy."

I recalled another night before the Tang scenario whilst I was still staying at the Villa with Don. He had taken a Vietnamese and a Khmer girl home for some fun-for-three. I always kept the entrance to my place closed so nobody could walk up from the flat downstairs. Whilst watching television one early evening, I nearly jumped out of my skin when this girl waltzed by me wearing a shirt belonging to Don and I didn't know who she was or how she had gotten into my apartment. I stuck my head out my door calling, "Don, are you there?"

I got no reply and sat down again.

A few minutes later the lady walked by me again.

I asked her, "Where is Don?"

She didn't even glance at me and proceeded to walk around. I didn't pursue any further dialogue, but it left me to think about how she got into the premises.

I spoke with Don later that night and he told me he had given her a key for downstairs. "Isn't it great, he went on to tell me, she had taken all my laundry, cleaned the place, and now she was off to the night market to buy food and didn't even need to ask her. What do you think Loc?" he asked, "If we pay her $50 a month, she will keep the place clean and do the laundry."

I didn't even think twice and said, "No not for me thanks, but if you want to hire a housemaid better to have a woman who could do that job and she is over fifty years of age and who you won't be sexually attracted to."

The following day Don told me, "That fucking bitch stole my electric iron and water container. The iron cost around $20 and for the container you got a $4 deposit on return." Don laughed whilst commenting, "Now I know what they mean when they call them *taxi girls* but it should be *taxing you* girls!" He laughed until tears were in his eyes.

KAMPOT

The motorbike driver whom I often used was going to see his mother who lived in Kampot. He had told me he hadn't visited her at Khmer New Year and he wanted to visit her now. I went along with him on the back of his motorbike we arrived in Kampot my new friend dropped me off and then he went to see his family. I was planning on staying for four days so I told him we would meet back in Sihanoukville.

I hadn't been keeping up my meditation practice this was mostly due to being distracted by my new spirit companion. I thought this trip away was the ideal time for me to sit in meditation again.

Bodhi Villa guest house sits on the bank of a river, one of many running through that region. I checked in and had a bamboo hut with a shower and toilet, plus a small outdoor sitting area. I put my bag down locked my door and headed to the front of the establishment. I went to where the bar was located seeing travellers hanging out and by the pungent smell in the air, they were smoking marijuana or just watching the river flow.

I met the owner at the bar who was an enthusiastic young Australian man called Hugh, he welcomed me with the typical Ozzie greeting of, "Gidday Mate."

Hugh then offered me a vaporizer the ultimate way to smoke your marijuana. I inhaled this offering from Hugh and enjoyed the flavour of the THC at its purist. It certainly was a laid-back place and I didn't venture further than my room to the bar area for a couple of days.

I was introduced to two brothers who came from Scotland, one of them was living in the property next to the Bodhi Villa. The two brothers had opened an Internet shop and assisted in establishing a school for the poor. I went to visit the school that they were sponsoring one morning with the elder brother Richard. While I was at the school Don texted me a telephone number and asked me to check it out as the owner had land for sale in Kampot at $15,000 a plot. Don had spoken to me on a few occasions that he would like to open a holistic retreat. I was beginning to sense that he was becoming sick and tired of his unhealthy lifestyle. I wasn't optimistic but this gave me hope.

I called the number but the person on the other end couldn't speak English. I returned to Bodhi Villa hoping to get someone to help me with asking questions regarding the land for sale. I spoke with Hugh he gave my phone to his staff member to ask for the location then he wrote it down on a piece of paper. Hugh suggested going onto the road and stopping a passing motorbike driver and giving him the address. As it happens this is a common occurrence in Cambodia to stop motorbike drivers and pay them for dropping you off someplace.

Of course, not all are willing to stop but fortunately, this one did and he also spoke English. I asked him if he could take me to this address and handed him my phone. He dialled the number and spoke with the person on the other end. I got onto his motorcycle. Hok was the driver's name and he was helpful and smiling and took me to the place to meet this person. We were met by a well-dressed man in his forties called Sovan, and a woman who wore large framed sunglasses and her hair tied up held in a gold clasp with large gold earrings to match. I immediately recognised by their attire and big car that they were wealthy.

We shook hands and he showed me the land area. It looked like a good location to me with a waterfront view. I explained to him, I was looking on behalf of my friend. It was when he handed me his name card it nearly dropped from my hand. It said, 'United Nations Office on Drugs and Crime'.

On impulse, I told him that I had exhibited paintings for the United Nations to commemorate their 10th anniversary of The World Anti-drug Day on June 26th in Shanghai China. I went on to say that it was 40 posters I had painted, done in four parts Cultivation and Distribution, Tools Used and Abused, The Anti-Drug Fight, and Prevention of Spreading AIDS.

Sovann the UN worker appeared to be impressed. It was then I dropped the bombshell telling him this exhibition had been done whilst I was serving a fifteen-year sentence for cannabis possession. Why did I blurt that out, being honest fucking John, this meditation was opening me up in ways I was not sure I wanted.

Sovann asked me if I would be interested in doing some work here regarding drug education.

I replied, "Let me think about that."

He told me to keep in touch and then they drove off.

The world works in wondrous ways and I had a beaming smile on my face. It was at that moment the soil held my feet to the ground again. It was a similar feeling that I experienced upon my arrival in Cambodia. I was being rooted into the soil.

The vision of the little girl jumped to the forefront of my thoughts and it jolted me. I reached out to hold onto the shoulder of the driver then came out from a momentary trance to my senses.

"Sir," he said, "are you okay?"

"Sure, I am fine." I still felt somewhat shaken.

Hok then told me his friend had land for sale, "Do you want to see Sir?"

I said, "Okay, let's go."

So off we went.

It was a nice feeling sitting on the back of a motorbike, the warm air brushing my face and taking in the sights. It wasn't that far. We turned onto a dirt path and went down there for several minutes then we came out at the riverfront. It was a great location but it had no road access other than the dirt path we had just come down.

I asked about the price.

It was just less than one acre in size and his friend wanted a third of the price for this place in comparison to the previous one. The old man who owned the land came out to meet us. I could see the suffering and hardship in the old man's eyes. It looked as if his tanned lined face came out from the ground across his brow looked like dried dug-up clay.

I thought for a few minutes then said to Hok, "Let me think about it," and that I would mention it to my friend.

Hok only lived five minutes away from the riverfront property and invited me to his house for a drink. I went along with him he was a genuine local man helpful and friendly.

At his house, I tasted his home-brewed rice wine out of courtesy but declined his offer to purchase some. Hok dropped me off at Bodhi Villa and I handed him $5 he looked at the money and said, "No Sir."

I insisted and put it into his hand then asked him to give me his phone number which he did. I told him that I would call him when I returned to Kampot and thanked him saying goodbye.

It was a good feeling sitting at the Bodhi enjoying a lovely chickpea salad, drinking a mango shake, and listening to music. It was now time for a vaporizer. I was hot and stoned and dived into the river to cool down. A few other travellers joined me splashing around and enjoying the tranquillity of our surroundings. I sat at the restaurant until late that night listening to music and chatting with the other guests. I went to my hut and slept soundly until morning.

I returned to the restaurant for breakfast and smoked a few more vaporisers and then lay on a hammock for a few hours. I finally unfolded myself - I saw on the table a book called *Siddhartha*. I remembered reading it thirty-odd years back when searching for the meaning of *me*. Now here I was sitting at a river at the Bodhi Villa - is that profound or what? I looked at the river, took a slow intake of air through my nostrils to fill my lungs, and then held it.

I exhaled slowly through my mouth and then repeated this breathing exercise several times until my eyes gently closed. The simplicity of sitting in silence is the outcome of the stilled mind. I was now unattached to how wonderful the river looked with closed eyes. Plop, the sound of a fish jumping in the water, my eyes darting in that direction, distracting me from my meditation.

AT MY DOORSTEP

I lay on the tiled floor in my shop, trying to keep myself cool as the heat was suffocating and the monsoons had already begun. It was often sunny outside at times causing the humidity to keep my skin in a constant state of stickiness. I lay thinking of what Andrew the press reporter had told me; about the case he covered on a celebrity paedophile. He had suggested to me to keep my ears to the ground and eyes open and if uncovering something sordid to contact him. Andrew had said you can earn some money doing this and advised me to drink juice instead of water when going into bars. He elaborated by saying drinking water is like telling the people at the bar you have a sexually transmitted disease.

This pop star paedophile topic had resurfaced, first of all at the Gang Hut in Glasgow and now here in Cambodia. It got me thinking of what a French guy called Napp had told me the previous week about letting children into my shop.

We had been drinking tea and he asked, "Why do you always leave the shop door open?" He continued, "What about that guy sitting over there? He comes around here two, sometimes three, times each week with children their age from eight to ten years old. Why do you allow that bastard to come and sit outside your shop?"

I replied, "He comes here most days what's your problem?"

"That bastard is a paedophile," he exclaimed, "or why would he come to Cambodia and only surround himself with children?"

It surprised me to hear these accusations and was about ready to tell him to fuck off and not stir up trouble.

Napp got out of his seat and started to abuse this guy in French, then again in English the guy sat there and didn't respond. Napp came back and said "What man would allow you to call him a paedophile and not attack you? That bastard is a paedophile," he fumed.

Napp had been living in this part of the world for twelve years and was the most down-to-earth guy I had met so far on my travels in Cambodia, maybe he had a point that I was missing.

I lay around that evening directly under the fan and often went for a shower to cool down. I eyeballed myself in the mirror, my head was shaved and the little girl from the cave appeared right behind me reaching up to take my hand.

The words echoed in my ears repeatedly saying that bastard is a paedophile. It was becoming quite a regular occurrence, this feeling of being directed towards revenge for something that didn't happen to me. I was often having flashbacks to my childhood reliving the memories of being sent into care homes and residential schools. It got me thinking as a child that something happened to me in one of those places and that had I erased it from my memory.

I started to think about that newspaper article I had done with Andrew it hadn't drawn enough attention for anyone to donate to what I had thought to be a worthy school project. I concluded that this little girl spirit who had been haunting me was here to tell me the best solution to help was to kill sex offenders. It was all finally coming together. That would be my contribution to the Cambodian children. After all, I had already taken matters into my own hands on a couple of occasions, although I hadn't given it much thought at the time.

Teaching English and art wasn't stopping the sexual abuse. The sponsors at the Hemphouse Shop in Glasgow were the only humanitarian souls reaching out to help me, in this broken land. It was just enough money to suffice, but not enough to help people change their life. There was this feeling surging through me accompanied with the spirit. It should be my responsibility, to take on the retribution for the abused children. I hadn't completely ignored the child spirit but I had certainly thought she was occupying too much of my time. Maybe I was wrong and should have been giving her my full attention.

.oOo.

I checked my email whilst in town and there was one from Andrew in Bangkok telling me that the policeman his friend was going after was found dead in his room and how he had died a horrible death. I didn't reply and never mentioned anything about that email to Don not wanting to arouse any further inquiries from his inquisitive mind.

Don had returned to Thailand again and would be gone for a couple of weeks. I was mostly painting every day until my mind became more preoccupied with a lady from a Pho Vietnam restaurant in town. I began returning to the restaurant every day and talked with this lady and discovered she was single but had two children. I was certainly interested in having a relationship with a mature woman her age 38 and pursued that avenue. I started by teaching her two children English every day in exchange for a free meal this arrangement was accepted by both parties and the children responded very well. I wanted to make a move on her in some sort of way but felt I didn't have the financial security to support a family.

I could sense tension coming from her through my lack of showing any intimate interest. One day she said to me in her broken English why you do not have a girlfriend? Do you like Ladyboy? It was time for me to move on she wanted a commitment to a relationship and I couldn't supply that so stopped going there but still liked Pho and her two children very much. I did have a conversation that evening with my spirit companion. I was advised by her that getting involved with someone would distract me from my commitment to her and that love wasn't part of my life that was needed.

I told her to go back to her grave and what in the world would she know about love or what I needed. That statement had annoyed her the whole night until morning doors were opening and shutting and I could hear pots rattling in the kitchen.

.oOo.

Don got back to Sihanoukville and came to visit me. He had spent a couple of weeks travelling through parts of Thailand to visit Nok's family. I could see a weariness in his eyes and mentioned to him that he looked very tired, he replied he was glad to be back at the Villa to rest.

Don asked me to make some Ginseng coffee for him and produced a large bag of this stuff, it gives me a lift every time he said, "Why don't you try one Loc."

We sat outside and he told me parts about his travels, highlighting all the good parts and the *body to die for* stories, the *best sex I have ever had* he assured me. I had heard similar stories in the past from him but this was special he assured me.

I asked why he didn't bring Nok back with him. Don replied she might just be on her way she texted me and asked me to send her the travel fare. It had been something we had discussed in the past, living with a woman here in Asia.

It was on my mind to settle down with one, but Don said you don't need to settle for one when you can choose to have fun when you feel like it. Now maybe that Nok was coming to Cambodia that was a change of mind from him but a good one in my opinion.

As the days went by and into weeks, I asked Don about Nok as she hadn't arrived.

"Well, Loc," he told me. "When visiting Nok's family money went amiss $2000 along with that nice jewellery made especially for my daughter."

"What do you mean it went missing? Did you lose it?"

"Well," he went on, "I don't know. It could have been left in a hotel room or at her mother's place. You know me," he said. "I never was one for checking my money."

Whilst listening to his story I could tell he didn't want to believe that the missing money had anything to do with Nok or her family. I was thinking otherwise but kept that to myself.

It was a mind shift that Don hadn't fully taken yet, so I put it to him this way. I said, "A bar girl works for $40-50 a month, if she can get a customer to spend money on alcohol, she gets a small commission. If she gets a customer, she can usually earn another $20 to $30 a night, but the competition is fierce." I went on to say half of these girls might only get one or two customers a month if they are lucky. Then one guy walks into the bar takes a liking to one and treats her like a princess. "She is now staying in a good hotel, eating the best of food in seafood restaurants, drinking white wine, and having great sex, plus into the bargain being paid for it."

"What's your point?" Don interrupted.

I said, "The treatment you receive and the care they take of you is wonderful. To be spoiled by such a beautiful woman, but it is a fact and she knows by multiple experiences you will be moving on. You are not the first guy who has come into their lives and left them behind with hollow promises, said in tender loving moments or the ecstasy of sexual climax. There are so many men convincing or kidding themselves and the ladies that they are returning to meet up again and marry them."

I could see he wasn't taking in what was coming out of my mouth but in his eyes saw it was a wake-up call. I spent the night at the Villa, Don went out while I stayed indoors watching television.

The following morning, I noticed strange movements; my routine seldom ever changed being an early morning riser getting up at dawn. Upon opening the veranda door just got a glimpse of a young lady exiting from the front gate. Don was having fun again and just as I was about to go back inside, another appeared fleeing over the yard and exited the premises.

Later on, in the day when we were sitting having coffee in the kitchen, Don eventually got onto telling me he had two darlings in bed together last night, "Where else in the world for forty dollars can you get that?"

In the following days, one of the girls had taken to calling around she was doing his laundry and keeping the place clean.

Don was enjoying this, he was enthused telling me he woke up and the place had been swept, the dishes washed, and the laundry outside drying he smiled. I didn't have to warn him of the danger of having someone you just met as a live-in partner. Don knew the score after his experience with Tang and the electric iron and water container thief if he wasn't careful, it would cost him money or trouble or more likely both.

THE MINISTER OF CULTURE

I had a vivid dream and woke dripping in sweat disoriented and my room was cold. I reached over and turned on the table light. I wiped the sweat from my face and body with the bedsheet still shivering and lay back down. In my dream, I was on a boat going down a river and had my baggage with me, in the front of the boat were a few children. The sky above me was orange and the sun appeared to look like a monk with a shaved head. The little girl sat right at my side holding a garrotte and smiled, then whispered, *it is time for revenge again*.

It was a clear message that I should remove myself from this town and go back into a meditation retreat away from this spirit.

I went over to the Villa and sat with Don telling him that I was leaving and would be giving up my place. Don asked why the sudden rush to leave Sihanoukville. I answered mostly for the change of scenery and left it at that.

Don asked, "When do you plan to leave?"

"I will pack my things up and head out of here in a day or two and put a notice on the board at Ana Internet that my place is now available for lease."

I headed out to Kampot a few days later and stayed at the Bodhi Villa again it was so peaceful there. I made some inquiries from the local staff about places for rent and was told to go into the town and visit some of the foreign-run establishments as they often had knowledge or signs up on their wall. After a few days of looking around and having no success, I met up with Richard the Scottish guy I had met on my previous visit. Richard told me the property next to him was empty and took me over to have a look at it.

We entered the place from the river, climbed onto the bank, and looked around. It was a great location and had a two-bedroom wooden house with a thatched roof on it with a separate brick kitchen and toilet at the back. I asked Richard who the owner was and he told me it belonged to the ex-minister of culture and that he lived in Phnom Penh.

I asked, "Do you have any phone number or address on how to get in touch with him?"

Richard told me that one of the locals came to the house once a week to maintain the grounds and that he would ask him for a contact number the next time he visited.

We went back to Bodhi Villa together and sat chatting for a couple of hours and exchanged phone numbers. Richard said he would be in touch as soon as the guy came back to clean the grounds. I wanted to go into town and Richard offered to take me on the back of his motorbike.

"If you plan on staying here," he suggested, "you might want to buy yourself a means of transport."

Richard took me to the market where they sold second-hand motorbikes and I bought one, paying $400. I now had to take the bike with me. I had only ever driven one in Thailand which I had rented for a day and wasn't a confident driver.

A few days later I got a call from Richard and he told me to meet him at his house which was only a few houses down from Bodhi. I didn't take the motorbike and just walked still not confident about driving. I met up and he gave me the address of the house owner but no phone number. Richard was a very helpful guy and suggested that we both go to Phenom Penh together the following day.

The following morning Richard said we had better fill our tanks up with gasoline before setting off.

"Are you serious?" I spoke. "No way am I driving that long distance."

Richard said, "Then jump onto the back of my bike."

So that's what I did and off we went.

The journey took around six hours, stopping at makeshift roadside tea shops to stretch our legs and drink some bottled water. We arrived around 4 am and I was thankful I didn't take my bike; the traffic was pandemonium. We checked into a guesthouse and cleaned up before going for something to eat. That evening we went into town. Richard drank a few beers whilst I reminisced about what had happened the last time, I was here. It wasn't pleasant thoughts but lingering in my mind was the pleasure I had felt ridding society of a serial sex offender. It was decided we would go and visit the ex-minister the following day.

Richard and I headed to the address which he had gotten from the guy who maintained the Minister's house. I could hardly believe my eyes, driving onto the premises. It was massive and had old Buddha statues and other incredible stone and wood carvings strewn across the garden. There were several buildings and we didn't know which one was the house that he lived in. Richard stopped and asked one of the groundskeepers to give us directions which he did.

We arrived at a beautiful building that looked like a palace for a King and we were greeted by an old lady who escorted us in. Richard and I looked at each other, our eyes wide open in awe.

Fifteen-foot-tall statues of deities surrounded the interior. There were intricate wood carvings of the Kama Sutra on the panelling that covered the walls and the furniture was majestic.

As we stood there looking at the amazing surroundings an elderly old man came out from behind a curtain and welcomed us asking how he could be of assistance.

The housekeeper entered the room and beckoned us to follow, she took us outside into the garden where she had placed a pot of tea. We sat down, and both Richard and I commented on the beauty of his abode and told him we came from Scotland and what our names were. The Minister hadn't introduced himself yet and we didn't know how to address him.

He then spoke asking, "Why are you in Cambodia?"

Richard told him he was working with underprivileged children teaching English and computer skills. I said my reason for being there was to go into a monastery for a ten-day meditation retreat but had decided to stay longer to assist with education with the orphan children.

I could see in his eyes that he wasn't impressed and looked at us somewhat suspiciously. "How can I be of assistance to you," he inquired.

I asked if his house in Kampot was for rent. I informed him that I wanted it mostly to be used as a place to live and also to use as my studio to open a gallery to display my art. I saw his eyes widen a little when I mentioned art.

The old man said his house might need some minor repairs and if I wanted, he could arrange for that to be done. We sat for another hour or so and eventually came to the agreement that he would rent me the house for $100 a month. We shook hands and he informed me that the monthly payments should be handed over to the groundkeeper. I suggested that I pay six months in advance but he shrugged me off saying just give the rent to the ground keeper. He then gave us a guided tour around the property.

I had never seen or could even imagine such a paradise could be found in the centre of town. It had a music auditorium and rows of bungalows for guests. It was abundant with fruit trees, and flowers of every size and colour. As we left the premises the old lady handed us his name card.

We returned to the guesthouse and then went out to eat. I was elated with the outcome of our visit; Richard and I chatted happily and would return to Kampot the following morning. We went out that evening and visited a few girly bars. The poster sign that I had seen in Battambang with the young girl walking hand in hand with a man going down a side street was in large print on the street outside the bar we went into. A sudden invasion leaped into my soul a reminder from the little girl that she was still with me. "Fuck off, will you," I spurted out involuntarily.

Richard looked at me and asked, "What did you say?"

On impulse replied that I had just remembered I needed to buy some art materials and would not be returning with him tomorrow.

"Okay," he said.

Then thinking what the fuck just happened to talk out loud to someone who was only in my head. I had often spoken with this spirit but only in the confines of my mind or room and rarely out loud.

BLANK CANVAS

The following morning after breakfast Richard took off back to Kampot and I headed out to the Russian market to buy some paints and canvas. On my way there I went into a bookstore and bought a city street map and guidebook. I knew that the reason for staying was solely related to this girl spirit who had now been urging me to take more action in revenging past abuses. I sat down at a noodle stall and opened the guidebook to find some direction to a museum or other place that would have history on the atrocities that had befallen this land. As I started to flip over the pages, I stopped and looked at a photo of the mountain of skulls.

I stared at that photo it took me back to the cave in Battambang. I felt a small hand touching my shoulder, her little voice whispered *this is not the place to look, the dead families and those children have passed onto another life; it is the living children you must protect.*

The lady at the restaurant picked up my empty bowl then suddenly she dropped it onto the ground. It was like she had burned her fingers and she turned her back to me as if she had heard or seen a ghost.

I was taken aback by her sudden reaction but continued to read my guidebook. I instinctively knew she had seen or felt something when looking at her facial expression. The little girl was close by but I ignored her presence. I put the book down and paid the vendor for my noodles and bottle of water. I could see something in the woman's eyes she wanted me away from her stall.

As I walked along the street speaking to the spirit in my head, I asked her why she was bothering me if those dead in the killing fields were in the past.

My mind exploded when her reply was, that she had been sexually abused and murdered by a Khmer Rouge soldier and buried among the skulls at the cave. The spirit girl was insistent letting me know that I had been chosen to prevent this atrocity from happening to other children. The word 'chosen' was reverberating around my head. Chosen by whom?

I hurried back to my room, lay on the bed after taking a cold shower started to go through the events of my arrival in Cambodia. I got the memory of the ground attachment then at the cave after leaving the monastery, the chicken shack scenario. It was scene-by-scene visions that appeared in my head the Conrad confrontation up until garrotting the pervert cop.

I then fell into a troubled sleep. It was dark outside when I awoke and my mouth was sour and dry and had the strong urge to visit a nightclub called Heart of Darkness which was once managed by Brian the Scottish guy. It was like my body was being guided and I headed there without haste.

Upon entering the place, the music was loud with people dancing wildly. Going over to the bar I ordered a beer and a shot of vodka with ice. It was a total out-of-body experience as if floating above the crowd. I knew that I was losing control and reverting to my old habits. I was trying to drown out my thoughts with alcohol. The last encounter with the spirit girl was stressful and overwhelming. I felt the need to obliterate her from my mind.

It was only minutes later that I was approached by a young lady, she asked me, "Where do you come from mister?"

I replied, "From the United Kingdom."

" Do you want to smoke with me?" she asked.

"Okay, without giving it a second thought replied, "Let's go."

And she led me outside.

"We go to your hotel, okay mister?"

I took her to the guesthouse and she produced a glass pipe and we started smoking crystal meth. It was instant euphoria and my body and mind took off. I lay on the floor with a clown-like grin on my face and stared at the ceiling for what seemed like hours. I eventually got up gave the girl some money and told her goodbye.

"Sir, you do not want sex with me?"

"No," my voice had an urgency to it, and half pushed her out of the room.

I lay there until the sun came up; my fucking head was bouncing off the walls. I couldn't even attempt to work out what had just happened. From not drinking alcohol, directly onto beer and vodka then smoking crystal meth with a hooker in my room. "I'm fucking deranged. I finally concluded that being possessed by this spirit was causing my mental health to deteriorate. I didn't have any ideas or solutions on how to resolve my problem. A voice in my head told me to run, hide, and escape thus reverting to the only thing I knew that would blank out my mind temporarily but also knew that it was just as harmful.

.oOo.

I left the guest house around midday and returned to Kampot. I travelled by bus; my head was fuzzy with the chemical residue from the alcohol and crystal meth. I was trying to recollect what had brought on the events of the night before that could account for my irrational behaviour. When I arrived at the Bodhi Villa the sun had already set. I went directly to my room and rolled myself an extra fat joint to give me an altered state from my present mindset. The room was dark and it made me feel secure. My body was tense and the muscles in my jaw felt as if they had been wired. I lay on the bed for some time then the sound of music from the bar took me out of my trance state. I got out of bed, sat on a chair by the window staring at the night sky, then returned to bed and slept.

The following morning sitting crossed legged in my room I began slow breathing exercises. My attempt to meditate wasn't successful, my thoughts kept jumping from one scenario to another returning back to the hooker in my room, or to the spirit girl.

I planned to visit the ground keeper and collect the keys from him after my morning coffee. I went to Richards's house and he took me to meet the groundkeeper. I picked up the keys and paid him $100 then moved into my new abode that afternoon. I swept all the floors then took the mattress from the bed and placed it outside to get fresh air and sun. I then went downstairs to the kitchen and toilet and threw buckets of water over that area. I would need to buy some toiletries and took some mental notes of things to buy in town.

It was wonderful sitting on the veranda looking directly onto the river. I returned to Bodhi Villa packed my bag and went to pay my bill, the owner Hugh was delighted to hear about me renting the place two lots down and asked me if he could be of any help to let him know. I got onto my motorcycle and dropped my bag off then headed directly into town to buy some household utensils.

Kampot is a very small town it has a thriving market with stallholders selling fruit, vegetables, and a good variety of hardware shops. I parked my motorbike and then went looking for a cooker, and gas bottle, plus I needed to buy some pots, plates, cups along with cutlery. I left some of my purchases at the shops telling them I would collect them later. It took me a couple of hours before I realised that I wouldn't be able to take all my shopping back to the house at once. I was told by one of the stallholders she could rent me a car so that is what I did after loading up my wares the driver followed me to my house.

Now sitting on my veranda after putting the plates along with the utensils into the kitchen. I rolled a joint then sighed with relief a feeling of settlement just puffing away my stress. I then realised that I hadn't bought any bedding but nothing was going to deter me; I would be contented lying on the bed half naked secure in the knowledge that I had my place. I decided to make a cup of tea then realised I hadn't bought any. I went over to Bodhi Villa to eat and smoke some good marijuana from Hugh's vaporizer.

That night I slept well at my new riverside house; it was magical and it was a beautiful location.

.oOo.

After I had been living at the house for three weeks and settled in feeling comfortable, I stocked up with snack foods, fruit, and bottled water. The next thing on my agenda was to get a large sign made to put near the roadside to let people know that an artist was in residence. I decided it would be called *Blank Canvas*, as it was a new beginning a fresh start - a clean sheet so to speak.

I phoned my friend Hok whom I had met on my previous visit and told him my house was next to Bodhi asking him if he could visit me whenever he had free time. Hok arrived shortly after my call he was delighted to hear about my plan to live in Kampot. I asked him about any place in town that made shop signs to put on the land near the road. Hok told me to jump onto the back of his motorbike and he took me to a shop to have my sign done. I wrote *Blank Canvas* onto a piece of paper at the shop and gave the sign measurements to the guy, which were twelve-foot high and five feet wide plus the font style and black lettering with a white background.

Whilst there at the shop the owner asked do you have a frame to mount your sign onto? He then sketched what would probably be needed to support the sign. Hok was doing all of the talking and he told me the guy wanted to visit the house to look at what materials he would need. The three of us returned to my place and the guy measured it up. Hok explained, first of all, he will need to dig a hole to put the concrete in to support it for strength. I asked how much will cost me. Hok chatted with the guy and then told me $150 which includes the sign, materials, and the labour to put it up. I agreed and we shook hands, he said he would return in a few days and left.

We sat and chatted for a while and Hok suggested to me to get a maid. It will be better for you to have someone go to the market and do my cooking and keep the place clean he advised. Do you have someone in mind I asked? Hok said to come with him to his house and I will introduce you to a lady. Hok and I went to his place and he introduced me to the lady who would become my maid. I thought this might be a bit of a problem and asked her do you speak English?

She replied, "Just a little sir."

Looking at her and thinking about the advice I had given Don in Sihanoukville. This lady fitted the profile perfectly, she was small in stature, slightly plump, with a plain face, and her skin colour was clearly of someone who was constantly under the sun working.

"What is your name?" I asked.

"Shea Sir."

"And how old are you, Shea?"

"My age is 42 Sirs."

Then asking Hok how much I shall pay as a salary each month and he replied without hesitation $50.

I agreed to employ her and she would come to the house the next day.

I smiled at her and she said, "Thank you Sir."

Then Hok drove me home. I handed Hok some money when we arrived at my house but he declined.

A few days later in the early morning, I heard the maid talking outside the front of the house. I went down from the veranda and saw the workers putting up the Blank Canvas studio sign. It was a moment of elation to see the sign being erected.

Shea made them some tea, happy to be helpful. It took a few hours and the job was completed. I paid the guy the remaining money owed to him. I asked if he could build me a couple of wooden easels but knew he didn't understand what I was saying. We went down to the house and I drew him an image of what was required.

The guy took out his phone he called Hok, then handed the phone over to me. I spoke for a couple of minutes then handed him the phone back. Hok had told me sir, he can make them for you but asked us both to come to his shop tomorrow is that ok? I said no problem. My sign was up and I was ready to open my doors to welcome visitors.

TWO VISITORS

Blank Canvas Studio hadn't had any visitors since putting up the sign. I was under the house painting the Prisoners Abroad logo on the wall when someone called out, "Hello, can we come in?"

Turning my head, I saw a young couple walking towards me.

"Sure," I replied, "welcome."

They introduced themselves, the lady was called Roza and her companion shook my hand and said his name was Duka. It was a Saturday morning and the maid didn't work at the weekend so, I asked them to sit upstairs while I put on water to make tea. Duka was blond-haired strong jawline he looked like his age was in his early 30s whereas Roza had tanned skin slightly slanted eyes long thick wavy black hair and was also in her early 30s.

I could immediately tell they weren't from a native English-speaking country by the way they spoke. I introduced myself and asked what country they came from.

Duka told me he was born in Moscow and Roza was from Kazakhstan.

Duka pointed to the marijuana on my table and asked is it okay if we have a smoke?

"Please do, help yourself!"

He proceeded to roll up a joint. We sat and smoked then Duka asked me where he could buy some marijuana. I told him that I got mine at Bodhi Villa.

He replied, "We were on our way there and saw your sign and came inside to have a look."

Roza asked me about the painting I was doing on the wall as they entered, saying that she had recognised the logo.

"I doubt if you would know that logo," I said.

"Why is that?" she looked at me surprised.

"It is an organization that helps prisoners abroad," I told her.

"Oh, I see. Do you work for them?" she asked.

"I don't work for them but I was a prisoner abroad in China from 1991 until 2003, for possession of cannabis resin."

Duka didn't show any surprise whilst inhaling the joint that he had just rolled.

Roza asked me about my experience in jail but told her it was too long a story maybe next time we could discuss that if you want to visit again. I asked them, "What are you doing in Cambodia?"

Duka said, "We are just travelling, but also looking for another country to settle down in. We both want to live in Asia."

"What sort of job do you have to sustain yourselves if you settle here?"

Duka explained that he taught martial arts and therapeutic massage. He asked, "Do you think there would be many opportunities here for that sort of work? I also have expert computer skills mostly on the dark web."

"The dark web? What is that?" I inquired.

Duka replied, "Maybe we can discuss that if we meet again."

"What about you Roza what sort of work do you do?"

Roza went on to tell me that she was a lawyer, and mostly worked overseas. She listed some jobs she had undertaken. I couldn't take it all in, she told me that she had worked for the

International Criminal Tribunal, also a Former legal at the Special Court for Sierra Leone, and the International Centre for Non-Profit-Law since 1992. Her resume was impressive, to say the least. Roza went on to say she recognised the logo on my wall because she also corresponded with them regarding human rights abuses in prisons worldwide.

I showed them around my house and we sat talking and smoking joints for a couple of hours. Roza suggested that we go to Bodhi Villa and have food together.

On the way to Bodhi, Duka asked, "Do you have classes we could join?"

"I don't hold classes, but you are welcome to come anytime you want," then told him the walls under the house were a blank canvas for anyone who wants to paint on them.

We arrived at Bodhi and were welcomed by Hugh. As we entered the premises Hugh said to me with a smile on his face, "Do you want a vaporizer man?"

I declined still feeling stoned from the session at the house, but Duka and Roza participated and we sat on the floor cushions facing the river.

As we waited on our food to be served, my new friends drank some cold Angkor beer while I had water.

Roza seemed to be preoccupied with the Bodhi Villa structure and kept turning her head and looking up. It was then she proclaimed that spirits were living nearby. -

That took me aback and I asked, "What do you mean by that?"

Roza explained the separation of the soul from the body, which is the ending of life. "When death is sudden and totally unexpected, you may find that you and your family members react in ways that seem strange." Roza continued that during her time in Sierra Leone, she had been contacted by them on numerous occasions and that she would pacify them with a silent prayer. "It is very strange," she went on to say, "I could also feel a presence in your house." She asked me, "Who is the spirit that lives with you?"

Fuck me, I nearly panicked thinking maybe she is psychic and will discover about the people that I had garrotted. My answer was that I had no knowledge of any spirit in my house but went on to say that when first putting my feet onto Cambodian soil it was like a magnet holding me firm to the ground.

Roza smiled and said, "Oh! You are a conduit for them to channel themselves onto the other side, or to move from one place to another."

I said, "Let's change the subject," feeling transparent and uncomfortable.

The food arrived and we all ate in silence, but inside my head, it felt like a debate was going on. I was once a criminal, a man who lived on the other side of the law but had intended to turn my life around by going to the meditation retreat.

It was now clear to me things had gotten out of hand since arriving in Cambodia it appeared life had other plans for me. After finishing our food, we returned to my house I told Roza and Duka about the meditation retreat and that I was looking for solace in the Buddhist teachings seeking redemption for my past transgressions. Little did I know that this journey would lead me down an even darker path.

On that fateful day, visiting the infamous Killing Fields the spirit was relentless she held control over my actions. I was desperate for help and reached out to Roza, who specialized in cases involving human rights violations and child exploitation. It was obvious to me that Roza had experienced spirit visitations after telling me about her communication with them overseas. I felt relief at being able to express what had been deeply troubling my mind heart and soul. I told them I had touched the skull of a victim, connecting my soul with that of a young girl's spirit.

Roza leaned forward on her chair her eyes opened wide as she stared into mine. I could see she was engrossed in my story.

I told them that my anger and pain consumed me, eventually overpowering me.

Roza told me to slow down. I was breathing heavily and beads of sweat had gathered on my forehead. I continued talking, controlling my thoughts telling them that revenge became her driving force as she manipulated me to seek out child abusers and paedophiles. While I wanted to believe these acts were justified, deep down I knew this wasn't the path of enlightenment.

I was expecting that Roza would tell me to meditate more but instead, she revealed to me what she knew about an underground network of paedophiles. Roza had already explained she had worked with the UN International Criminal Court.

Duka interrupted saying we are aware of their secret operations within South East Asia.

Roza then continued that she kept in touch with some friends in the UN.

I was taken aback when she told me that she had been informed that I was staying in Cambodia. I inquired as to how she could have known this.

Duka answered, "From the newspaper article that was available on the internet."

After my initial outburst and getting the stress from my mind, I held back, not revealing anything about my past actions. I began to feel suspicious about these two strangers who had just walked through my gate. I had a distinct sense that this couple had sought me out and that they knew more about me than they were letting on.

During that conversation, Roza revealed she was going to find work at any organization that dealt with wife and child abuse.

We formed an unlikely alliance, a partnership born from our shared opinions to bring these abusers to justice.

After they departed, I had another visit from the spirit girl. She told me that Roza knew about her presence at my house. She said Roza and Duka were reliable and could be trusted and that they also wanted justice for not only children but for all the abused. That reconfirmed what Roza had told me at Bodhi Villa about a spirit being present in my house.

I went over the day's conversation in my head. A lot had been said but nothing about my actions had been revealed. I was sure that their encounter with me wasn't accidental. They knew too much about my past. The first clue was Roza pointing out the Prisoner Abroad logo painted on my wall then Duka said he read my story on the internet. I still had no idea what their interest in me was but I was sure it wasn't coincidental.

A VISIT FROM DON

Don arrived at my house unannounced, he had gone to Bodhi Villa first and they told him about the Blank Canvas studio sign a few houses down. I had previously let him know about the place but he had arrived in Kampot from a different direction and wouldn't have seen the sign.

"How are you doing pal," he asked.

"All is well, I'm slowly but surely getting settled in here, would you like some tea or coffee?"

"Sure, Loc you know what my preference is black tea, no sugar."

I went down to the kitchen, putting on water to boil.

"I have some news for you," he smiled. "There are a couple interested in renting your old place. I spoke with them about the rent and fittings they are prepared to move in this week if you will accept $900."

I made a quick calculation in my head and said to tell them they could have it. For whatever reason, it didn't surprise me that he took the $900 from his wallet and handed it to me saying he would get it from them when handing over the keys. Don looked around the place and complimented me on finding such a serene watering hole then we went down to the waterfront to drink our tea. I told him about the couple who had visited and about the credentials Roza had. The first comment from my friend was, "Is she sexy.".

Jokingly I replied, "She has a body to die for," and we both laughed at that. I asked him if he was going to spend the night. He said he would.

That evening we went into town and ate at an Indian restaurant the food was authentic as the chef was from Bombay and had married a local lady.

Don asked him about any good bars in town to meet ladies. I am sorry mister there is no place like that here, only a massage house. He then winked at us both and said with a happy ending. We walked around the small town and saw a sign Irish Bar and went in to check it out. The owner was from Dublin and was living with his girlfriend who came from the seaside town Kep, which was not so far from Kampot. Don ordered himself a beer and asked me what I would like to drink. Don was inquiring about any property for sale or rent in town. Barry didn't have any idea but suggested looking around other foreign-run establishments, of which he said are only just a few. We sat for a couple of hours, questioning Barry about all sorts, trying to get as much information regarding the goings on in town.

We then headed back to my place and I mentioned to Don that the guy from the UN Anti-drug office who was selling land had told my friend Hok he has other land and I can arrange for him to take you there tomorrow if you want.

It was the middle of the night when Don came and woke me up, he told me the real reason for his sudden visit. Don said he had been talking with the French guy Napp on several occasions and then he had also started to take notice of the guy sitting with children at my old shop.

"I slashed him" Don blurted out.

I exclaimed, "Why did you do that?"

"He is a paedophile." Don explained, "While showing that couple your shop for rent, he had his hand on the little boy's knee.

I waited until the potential renters had left and invited him into the shop. I took a kitchen knife and stabbed him in the groin and ass, then slashed his face open. I think he has gone to the police and reported it so if you don't mind can I stay with you for a week?"

"Of course, you can you are always welcome here."

I reminded Don that the police wouldn't be that concerned. Nobody had been killed and if they ever did find the assailant their interest would be money and not solving a crime. Cambodia is corrupt I reminded him police salaries are low. I knew the system well enough some money-back hander to appease them would resolve the matter. Don smiled saying thank fuck we are not in the UK.

The following morning, I phoned Hok and he came to the house. I introduced him to Don, and asked if he would contact the guy from the UN and take him to the property, he had shown me.

"Yes, no problem, Sir," and off they went.

I sat around the house smoking marijuana and drinking tea. Shea had gone directly to the market to buy some fruit and vegetables, arriving back at the house around 10 am.

I asked her to cook rice and vegetables and also to make a fruit salad. I continued smoking joints and staring at the river from my porch, lost in thought thinking about ideas for a new painting.

Don and Hok arrived back around midday, and we ate lunch at my house. I then asked Don if he had any success in finding a piece of land.

"Not at all. The guy is asking too much money plus the ground was too soft and would be flooded every monsoon."

"How do you know that?" I asked.

"Hok told me," He replied.

"I am going back to Sihanoukville after eating," Don said.

"What about the story you told me? That the cops will be looking for you."

"Fuck it," he replied, "nobody saw me except the children, and they only heard the screams."

We shook hands and I thanked him for giving me the money for the shop, and for helping me to find someone to lease my old place. It was a short visit but good seeing my friend was still on the ball. I wasn't really surprised when listening to what my friend had done to the child molester, he still had that violent streak that resurfaced when needed and, in this case, it seemed appropriate.

.oOo.

After Don left, I met Duka in town, he was passing the shop where I was buying acrylic paints, and I called out to him. We shook hands and went to have a cup of coffee.

"Where did you meet Roza?" I asked.

"It's a long story," he exclaimed but went on to tell me. "We first met on the Internet. A friend of mine who is a computer hacker and who came across her profile whilst he was researching war crimes in Chechnya. He saw that Roza worked as a lawyer in similar cases."

"Oh, that sounds interesting," but I didn't get the connection.

Duka went into more detail telling me that he is part of a group that gathers information on war criminals and dishes out retribution to such offenders.

I suggested to him why don't you and Roza come to the house this evening and have a meal and smoke.

Duka agreed, shook my hand and we went our separate ways.

Whilst in town I picked up some cakes from a foreign-managed bakery that employed residents with learning disabilities, their bread and cakes were delicious and, although a little costly, were worth it. I got home and asked Shea to prepare food telling her some visitors were coming that evening. Shea's cooking skills were mediocre but all the ingredients were fresh and that would suffice.

Roza and Duka arrived just as the sun was going down and we sat at the river in silence smoking marijuana. I had mentioned my time in prison in China when we first met.

Duka then went on to tell me that they had read the article recently published in a Scottish newspaper, *Ex-Gangster Brings Karma to Cambodia Killing Fields*.

"Fuck me," I retorted are you a spy?"

Roza let out a laugh and answered, "Yes, he is but not for the government."

They both came to the kitchen and helped me to lay out the food then we went upstairs to the porch and ate. I wasn't sure if I should mention the murders in Battambang or Phenom Penh so, I danced around the issue. But I was starting to trust Roza and Duka, I felt that they were kindred spirits – and the spirit girl was nudging me to open up to them. When I first met this couple that night after they had left the spirit girl had told me to trust them. I had concluded that meeting them wasn't coincidental. I held back and inquired some more.

I asked Duka about the retribution against war criminals that he had touched upon when we met in town. Duka and Roza looked at each other and seemed to agree about something with a nod.

Duka said they both felt that I could be trusted.

It unfolded that Duka and some friends in Moscow hunted down war criminals online and passed on the offender's new assumed names and location to another group who dealt with what punishments should be meted out to them. Duka revealed that his mother's sister along with her husband and children had been taken prisoner in Chechnya. The husband had been made to do forced labour and his aunty and cousins were used as sex objects for the troops.

I was shocked by this revelation.

Duka expressed his loathing for these war criminals. Telling me that to continue with his revenge campaign he needed a safe haven and that in Cambodia, extradition was difficult to acquire if he ever was caught.

Roza, on the other hand, because she was a lawyer and worked in the UN had access to files of certain government officials who had turned a blind eye to atrocities going on around the world whilst they were in public service.

I knew that Roza carried high ideals from the stories she had told me whilst in Africa. It was her willingness to respect the existence of the universal truth and be responsible for the world around her. Roza had decided to assist Duka since they started a romantic relationship her insight and legal knowledge were a massive contribution to the group.

I asked, "What about here in Cambodia? What are you doing here?"

Roza said they were seeking out several retired officials from the Pol Pot era and would pass on whatever information they found to a group based here in Siem Reap.

I asked, "What that has to do with war crimes in Chechnya?"

Roza explained, "We are an international group, we reach out to help each other. There are no borders when it comes to heinous crimes imposed upon innocents."

I thought to myself, those officials must be elderly men now, but didn't say anything and just listened. It was a very interesting conversation and I asked them if they wanted to spend the night at the house. They both nodded in unison and we smoked some more joints, then chatted late into the night

I wanted to know more about the dark web and Duka explained that it uncovered a lot of wrongdoings in society.

"Can you give me some examples?" I was curious about this mysterious cyber world.

Duka started to explain it to me - that the dark web is easier to access because the deep web was encrypted - but I interrupted him when he used the word *encrypted* and said, "Just forget about explaining it to me knowing I would never understand.

In the morning we got up and sat around smoking marijuana and drinking tea.

I asked, "Have you heard much about the child abuse and sex trade here?"

Roza said sure and that she was going to be interviewed next week at a Non-Government Office that worked with assisting abused women and children.

I told them, "Since you both have been honest with me; I am also interested in doing something for the abused children here in Cambodia."

Roza seemed to think for a moment and then looked as if she had made a conscious decision and told me that the spirit of a little girl in your house visited me last night. Children who are emotionally traumatized because they are victims of violence or have died a violent death deserve special attention. Their lives are cut short so early and so brutally when they aren't ready to go, their traumatized spirits are bound to haunt the land of the living."

She looked deep into my eyes as if seeing both myself and the spirit, as she continued. "It isn't an unusual phenomenon for me, to see these spirits, in my job having to deal with murder and rape of people every day. It all depends on if you are open and receptive to the sufferings of others." She sighed and then went on, "And it is obvious to those lost souls that you are receptive or the little girl wouldn't be frequenting your house." She paused before adding, "Are you serious about wanting to help the victims and help this child spirit find peace?"

I burst out, "Yes."

It was all too much for me to take in though, and so I then changed the subject saying, "Shall we go to Bodhi for some breakfast? We can continue with this conversation later."

They went down to the wash area to brush their teeth and freshen up then we all headed out for breakfast. After eating Duka and Roza left to return to their guesthouse. We didn't make further plans to meet again but just waved goodbye.

I went to my bedroom and lay down my mind was a fangled mess of wild thoughts. I then got up and sat in the lotus position trying to empty my mind. It didn't work. I lay back down again and stared at the ceiling, my body was restless, out of sync, and losing touch with reality. I didn't eat or drink anything other than breakfast that morning.

I didn't sleep at all that night, my mind preoccupied by the visit from Don and Roza and what they had both told me. I had the feeling someone stood at the foot of my bed staring at me but knew exactly who that was. I didn't want to ruminate any further about what I had done or what I had heard from my new friends. At this moment I wasn't in search of an answer or to find relief from intrusive fear, doubt, and worry.

THE HIT LIST

I took my computer over to Bodhi Villa, to check if I had any emails and got one from someone, whom I didn't know. I wasn't very computer literate but had heard stories that some people sent viruses and if you opened the email the virus spread to all your contacts.

I called Hugh the proprietor over and asked him about it.

He said, "It is probably *spam*. Just delete it."

"Spam? What the fuck is spam thinking to myself?" I had never heard that word before – the only spam I knew to be a cheap processed food. I didn't give it much thought but curiosity got the better of me and opened the email. I was reading down the page and it didn't make any sense.

On the top of the e-mail, it said *Cambodia* with names under it, and then it said *Vietnam* with names under that. I closed the computer and returned to the house and was about to roll a joint when my mobile phone rang. It was Duka telling me that Roza had got the job in Phnom Penh and asked me if I had received an email from her.

I told him that I received an email from someone unknown but couldn't understand it.

Duka said he would come over to meet me at Bodhi before sunset and we could have a smoke and he would explain the email contents.

I arrived at Bodhi and Duka was sitting by the river staring up at the sky.

I said, "Hey, how are you, my friend?" and sat down beside him.

"All is good," he smiled and handed me the joint he was smoking. Duka asked me to show him the e-mail, but I had forgotten to bring my computer and told him to wait until I went back over to the house to get it.

"There is no need for that," he said, "use mine." As he handed me his laptop.

"I cannot use your computer - the e-mail is on mine."

Duka looked at me his lips twisted and his eyes looking up in bewilderment. Duka said, "You can access your email account from any computer."

"Really how is that possible?"

"It is how the system works, so just go to your account and log in, you can do it from anywhere in the world."

My first thoughts were this fucking dark or deep web hackers' shit and he wants to know my password. I was very suspicious and called Hugh to come over and help me.

"What's the problem?" Hugh asked.

I told him what Duka had told me and Hugh replied, "So what do you want to know?"

"I want to fucking know how I can access my email on his computer."

Hugh also looked at me and said, "Are you pulling my leg?"

"Not at all," Hugh shook his head and laughed, "You're fucking stoned brother. Haven't you noticed travellers come here to check their e-mail on my computer?"

As it happened, I did notice but hadn't given it any thought. I then asked, "But aren't passwords supposed to be secret?"

Hugh said, "They are. When you sign into your account nobody should be watching over your shoulder."

"Is it okay if I use your computer now?" I said, still not fully trusting to use Dukas.

"Sure," and he went behind the bar counter and handed it to me.

I followed his instructions and sure enough, I could read my mail. I knew this from using my computer then realised that I had done this several times before on a public computer at Ana Internet in Sihanoukville. I was stoned right enough.

I showed Duka the contents and he said let's go over to your place and talk.

As we left Bodhi; I waved my hand thanking Hugh for his assistance to which he replied get with it old man. On the way to my place, I realised it was a paranoia attack, Duka with all his talk about cyberspace, the dark web, and hacking.

Duka explained to me that Roza had sent me a list of women and their abusers.

I asked, "Why did she send the names of people in Vietnam though?"

Duka said he wasn't sure but she would be back in Kampot at the weekend and I could ask her then.

We spent a few hours talking about our past travels and experiences - he was a reasonable guy never trying to exaggerate his exploits or boost his ego. Duka suggested we return to Bodhi and eat, as he felt like getting some vodka. So, we went there around 10 pm, the music was in full swing and several foreigners dancing.

I accepted a vodka from Duka and that was the beginning of a wild drunken night, both of us staggering back to my place in the early hours of the morning. I immediately fell onto the bed still with my clothes on and slept.

The following morning, I was awoken by the maid calling, "Sir, would you like some tea?"

I said yes, then put my feet on the floor and got out of bed. I shouted, "Hey Man, time to get up!"

Duka joined me on the porch and proceeded to roll a joint. "What happened to you last night?" he asked. "I thought you didn't drink." He was smiling. Then said, "You can swallow vodka like a Russian sailor," and laughed at his comment.

I was not in such a joyous mood feeling the beginning of a hangover coming on fast. I went down to the washing area and took a cold bath, throwing water over my head and body. I returned upstairs feeling momentarily refreshed and drank my tea. Duka and I sat around most of the day and smoked without much conversation.

Shea had cooked some lunch and then she went home leaving me to fend for myself. I didn't have much of an appetite still having a fuzzy head.

Duka was going back to Bodhi, and I decided not to join him, before leaving he said, "Roza and I will visit you at the weekend."

I sat and rubbed my aching skull; my eyes were slightly bloodshot and out of focus and just lay on the bed nursing my hangover, I was slowly reverting to my old ways of alcohol and substance abuse.

.oOo.

The following morning Hok phoned me asking if I had free time? he wanted to discuss his school football team with me. Hok gave me directions and told me to turn right from my house and drive straight for a few miles and I would see a large, yellow-painted building on my left and to stop there. I arrived okay there was a group of young boys running about kicking a ball behind us. The ground was uneven and grass patches overgrew everywhere.

"So, is this your team my friend?"

Hok nodded in affirmation. He said, "We hope to be able to make a full team for the up-and-coming competition."

"When will that be?" I inquired.

Hok said he didn't have a date yet but usually, it would be held during the school holidays.

I asked, "What can I assist you with?"

Hok replied, "We need a sponsor to buy football strips and balls."

I told him to let me think about that, some friends of mine in Scotland might be interested in helping.

Hok asked me out of the blue, "Would you like to visit a brothel, sir?"

"No thanks," I said, taken aback by his suggestion.

He exclaimed, "Not to meet a girl just to show you what usually happens when teenage boys leave school and what some do when they earn some money. Some fathers recommend them to do this before taking a wife.

"What are you telling me Hok?" I looked at him inquiringly.

He replied that many fathers send their sons to meet girls for sex before getting married.

I thought this to be an unusual arrangement. It didn't fit into the vision I had seen or imagined. Firstly, the economics for most people was they were poor. I knew from what I had read, girls kept their boyfriends a secret from their parents. I had never seen young couples in the street holding hands. I quickly worked it out it must be or was another version of the Chicken Shacks I had seen in Battambang. I was completely taken aback hearing that some fathers recommended their sons to visit these dens of inequity.

That got my ears to perk up and I agreed to join him. We drove further into the countryside, on bumpy dirt paths, then stopped outside of a few dilapidated straw-thatched huts.

The sound of our motorbikes arriving brought a few ladies out - I guess they thought we were customers.

Hok talked to an elderly woman who was smoking a hand-rolled cigar, she had unkempt white hair and dirty clothes. I was looking at the girls, they looked between the ages of 16 to 20. I inquired from Hok, "Where are these girls from?"

He said, "Not from Kampot Sir, they come from villages further away."

"How do they get here?" I said inquiring further.

Hok said, "It is usually an uncle who brings them, or they have been sold by their parents to pay off debt."

This was becoming a familiar story to my ears and it was sickening to my soul.

On the way back we stopped at my house I said to Hok, "Doesn't this bother you that these young girls are being sold as sex slaves?"

Hok told me, "It isn't unusual here Sir, going on to say that he cannot prevent it from happening."

I was thinking it would be better to pay the debt to set a girl free than to sponsor football strips. "How much would it cost to pay off the debt for the girl to be able to return to her family?"

"That would not help sir, once the girl has been sold or rented, she cannot return to her village she would be an outcast."

Fuck me my mind and soul were spiralling out of control again getting palpitations, and I wanted to vomit. It seemed that these chicken shack brothels that I had first encountered in Battambang were everywhere. It was a clear part of the poverty lifestyle cycle and it appeared to be accepted by the people. I didn't think I would ever get my head around this rent-and-sell-your-children culture; it fucking disgusted me.

ACCOMPLICES

I got a visit from Duka and Roza on Saturday morning, we shook hands and went upstairs to my house and as usual, started to smoke marijuana. "How is your new job?" I inquired.

Roza said it was quite eye-opening. She continued to enlighten me regarding the abuses that had been reported to her office.

I immediately asked her about the e-mail she had sent to me.

Roza went on to explain, "There are some people who have been reported to my office. The offenses vary from rape, family abuse, and selling their children to pay off the debt they had accrued from gambling, along with other bad habits such as alcohol and drug abuse."

I asked, with an exasperated look on my face, and stood up rubbing my brow with the palm of my hand "Why are you telling me about this? Isn't it your office's job to assist these people?"

Duka replied, telling me to sit down "We are aware that you want to prevent abuse to children. As we also do."

I asked, "Are you suggesting that we take matters into our own hands?

Duka said, "We are certainly thinking about it."

There was a long pause, where I looked from Duka to Roza and back again. Their faces were sincere and they kept eye contact with me. I could tell that they had been thinking about it for a fairly long time.

"Does your office have photos of the people on the list you sent to me?"

Roza said she hadn't seen any.

Duka asked me, "What do you have in mind?"

I told him, "I don't have anything in mind."

Roza said, "If the case was reported to the police maybe they would have photos on file."

We spent most of the weekend together looking for a place to rent for my new accomplices. They had found a place in town and sorted out the rent arrangements, then Roza returned to her job.

On Monday afternoon, I assisted Duka in moving their luggage after he had checked out of their guesthouse. We went into the market area in town to buy some household accessories. Whilst there I said to Duka, "Let's meet my neighbour, Richard."

It was an opportunity also for me to see his computer shop, as I had never visited since my arrival. Richard was pleased to see me and immediately offered us a coffee. I then introduced Duka and mentioned that he was here with his girlfriend who was working in Phnom Penh.

They shook hands and we sat down. I saw a few young local Khmer people sitting at the computers and asked Richard what are they doing. Richard explained they were learning computer skills. "I am teaching them how to do spreadsheets."

Duka asked, "Do you have an internet connection set up?"

"Yes, why? Do you want to use it?"

"Sure, if you don't mind?"

So, Richard took him into another room and then he returned to continue our conversation.

Duka came back ten minutes later and asked Richard if he could print out a document for him. Richard obliged, it was printed out and handed over to him.

Duka asked, "How do I pay you for this service?"

Richard said, "It's okay, free this time."

Both of us thanked him and said maybe we could meet up at Bodhi sometime and buy him a beer. Then Duka and I headed to my place on the motorbike. As soon as we had sat down, he handed me the printed document and then proceeded to roll a joint, his favourite pastime.

I read the printout - it was more sexual abuse of children and was now clear to me paedophilia was a worldwide sickness. I put the document down went to the kitchen and made tea. Upon my return, Duka asked what I thought about it. I couldn't answer, my mind hadn't fully absorbed the contents.

After reading the document again and feeling sick in my stomach knowing about the abuses going on worldwide. I asked, "Where did you get this information?"

Duka looked at me then raised his eyes and said, "From the internet while you sat and spoke with Richard. I just wanted to show you that it isn't only in poor countries this sick degenerated behaviour goes on. It is all across the world. Religious organizations, people in Hollywood, and politicians are among the worst offenders."

I sat back and took a deep inhale of the joint Duka had passed to me and thought to myself, fuck me, the little girl's spirit was just the tip of the iceberg; it appeared there was still a mountain to climb and the avalanche was still to come.

.oOo.

Duka was spending most of his days at my house, he had started to paint a mural on my wall and was enjoying the process. I had started to work on a canvas of a monk standing alone looking into a mirror, but the reflection showed a ghostly image of a little girl holding his hand. That was me trying to portray what was going on inside my mind.

The weekend had come around again and Roza arrived holding a folder with several photos inside. She pointed out to me, "These are some of the offenders living nearby."

As I looked at them and saw that a couple lived in Sihanoukville, one lived locally and another one lived in Kep, which was not very far from Kampot. There was another name on the list who was Chinese and lived in a place called Poipet.

Roza mentioned that the Poipet area had the biggest number of abuses going on. This was due to it being transformed into a gambling and prostitution strip opened up by rich Chinese investors. The majority of abusers Roza pointed out from the list were all in the Phnom Penh area.

Roza and Duka left me to go into Sihanoukville, they were planning on buying new clothes and the selection in Kampot was limited but in Sihanoukville, there was a thriving black market with clothes coming across the border from Thailand. While they were gone, I sat with my spirit companion having a psychic conversation. The spirit always had the same agenda which was revenge. I gave some thought, on how to go about getting my hands on one of these abusers especially as I now knew some lived close by.

The nearest place to where I lived was a small town called Kep, it was around 30 kilometres away. I decided the best idea was for me to go there by motorbike and survey the surroundings. I had prepared a mantra written on a piece of paper OM MANI PADME HUM it is the sixth syllable mantra of Avalokiteshvara Chenrezig, the Buddha of infinite compassion. In my disillusioned mind, although I intended to kill a predator. I prayed that the receiver of this mantra would reincarnate into a more humane person. I silently repeated the mantra several times - in the hope that it would put the abuser onto the path with the intention and wisdom of the pure body, and speech to find a better Karma in the afterlife.

I knew in my heart there was no compassion in the spirit of the little girl and it was she who was my present guide. I folded the mantra along with a photo of the abuser and his address putting it into the pouch around my neck. I then got dressed in my Buddhist attire. I left my house at 6 am the following morning it took me an hour to get there but I had no idea of the area or where to look for the house of the paedophile.

I couldn't ask anyone for directions, or show a photo, for the simple fact that would give away my identity. I drove around looking at the names on the streets and to my utmost dismay, many of them didn't have any street names or numbers. It was still early morning and the day was young. I stopped at a restaurant in town and ordered a cup of tea and a loaf of freshly baked French bread.

It took about another hour before locating the address through methodically going street by street. I finally found his house on a quiet cul-de-sac with only eight other buildings that I could see. I drove past and then about turned and drove past again. The streets were beginning to get busy with schoolchildren. I decided to return to Kampot and would come back the following morning. Then on second thoughts I checked into a guesthouse and stayed in Kep for one night.

That evening I drove past the abuser's house again, this time there was a blue car parked outside. I didn't wait around and returned to the guesthouse to think over what could be done to meet this sicko bastard face to face.

I took out the A4 paper that Roza had given me it was his ID card with his photo - it also had his workplace address. I didn't know that location or have any clue in what direction to look.

Laying in my bed that night the little girl came into my mind she was silent with downturned eyes but she didn't give me any disturbing thoughts or messages. I had begun to realise that I had a duality disorder which only became obvious after numerous communications with the spirit. I had become separated into two or more distinct personalities.

I awoke to the sound of chirping birds outside my room window, then my dream came back into my mind. I had been walking across a road then being hit by a blue car knocking me off the roadside into a rice field.

I got out of bed, brushed my teeth jumped onto my motorbike, and drove to the abuser's house. As I was arriving a blue car was heading in my direction, the front of it was covered in mud. It was the same car in my dream. I turned around and followed it heading in the direction of Kampot. The car stopped at a factory building and I watched the driver get out. It was the abuser who was in the photo that Roza had supplied. I didn't intend to hang around all day outside the factory so returned to the guesthouse checked out and drove back to Kampot to plan for another day.

A WELCOME ADDITION

I had been getting regular visits from Duka and Roza there were always new stories about abuses. I found it very dark and often diverted the conversation onto lighter topics. Every time we met the new information was becoming overwhelming.

The latest news from Roza was about a little boy who had been raped and found dead in a field.

Then Duka was telling me about Hollywood paedophile rings that had been brought to light by child actors and actresses.

I suggested we go over to Bodhi Villa and have some refreshments in the hope the topic would change.

We entered Bodhi just as Hugh was opening a fresh bag of weed. I smoked a couple of vaporizers kindly supplied by the proprietor.

Duka and Roza had ordered beers with a snack of peanuts. The conversation about abuses carried on regardless of my efforts to divert it to lighten the load from my troubled mind.

It was just around sunset when Don walked in and smiled saying he had just come from my place and knew where I would be if not there.

I introduced him to my new friends and we all sat and had a nice meal courtesy of Don's kindness.

As the evening went into the night, Duka and Don were deep in conversation. It was obvious both were getting drunk. Roza and I smoked a few joints and she had the occasional vodka with lemon and ice from the other two who were in full swing.

Don asked my friends how long they were planning to stay in Cambodia. Roza told him she was working part-time in an NGO office.

I told Don she was a lawyer - information that got his attention - and he started to ask her more about her work.

Roza explained that she had worked for the UN and in what countries her services were required. They chatted for hours often resulting in Don's eyes widening at the information he was receiving.

When it got late, we decided to return to my place. Don and Duka still not satisfied with their alcohol intake bought a bottle of vodka and we all sat on my porch until the early morning. I went to my bed and Roza went into the other room leaving the other two to continue their drinking session.

When the sun came up, I went down to the waterfront. Don lay fully clothed sleeping on a bed without any mattress or pillow. The housemaid had arrived and started clearing away the empty glasses and sweeping the floor. I just sat on my porch drinking coffee and smoking joints until Roza got up and joined me.

It was later that morning everyone was awake and we sat chatting about some of the things we had discussed the night before. It came as a surprise to me when Don asked about the paedophile hunt. Both Roza and I looking at Duka gathered that during their drinking session, this topic had arisen.

There was an uneasy silence, and then Roza asked what do you mean?

Don continued, "Duka was telling me that you not only worked with the United Nations you are now doing work here uncovering war criminals and exposing abuses on women and children."

Roza confirmed that he was correct.

Don then offered to assist in getting payback on the abusers.

Duka said, "We could use all the help available!"

That was how a new and useful member of the paedophile hunters team became involved. I didn't make any mention of my visit to Kep.

Don left that afternoon along with Duka and Roza, we hadn't made any arrangements about getting together again. I just rolled another joint thinking about how all this madness came about. As sure as the sun rises every day the presence of my now regular companion reminded me that my mission in Cambodia was still ongoing. I was mumbling obscenities to myself, hoping she would hear my inner voice and leave me alone and haunt someone else. I just knew deep inside she had chosen me; she had picked someone vulnerable with a reoccurring addiction problem. I had thought I was fully in control but now understood I couldn't even sit in meditation for any length of time without her invading my thoughts. My great expectation to find enlightenment was just another illusion.

CRYSTAL METH

I had met a few people in Sihanoukville that used crystal meth, especially the girls of the night, and definitely, the Vietnamese woman whom Don and I met at Pet Lip Tours. Then one time down at the Frog Shack on the beach, I met a guy from Australia who was totally out of his mind on Ketamine. I had seen him a few times after that but didn't befriend him.

Then one afternoon out of the blue, he appeared at my house in Kampot, I greeted him and inquired as to how he knew I was there. He answered that he had been at Bodhi Villa and the owner told him. Tim went on to tell me he was delivering a few rocks of crystal meth to someone in Bodhi. We sat and smoked a few joints, then Tim got out his glass pipe and put in a small rock of crystal lit it then deeply inhaled and passed it over to me which I accepted without any hesitation. The meth smoke filled my lungs and a flash shot into my brain immediately giving me a rush and temporarily stopping my breathing.

Wow! Coming back from my lapse of reality exhaled what seemed to be for eternity, emptying my soul with the smoke into the air. Tim reached over and took the pipe from my hand. We took a couple of more puffs and Tim refilled the pipe. I sat there with a permanent grin on my face listening to Tim's adventures. There was one story in particular about how a monkey had come in through his window at his apartment in Phnom Penh and had chased him around his room while he was high on Ketamine. My brain was fried, some of the mad stories he told me were really out of this world, and in my present state of mind, I hadn't touched down to earth yet. The sun had disappeared, a deep red reflected from the water, and there was a warm inviting light on the walls of the porch. We continued to sit and smoke, having purchased a couple of rocks from him not wanting to be seen as not contributing to the two-man party. The night passed onto morning and as the sun rose, we both still sat smoking, lips glued to the meth pipe. Tim eventually got up from the chair and told me he was leaving as he had another appointment. I bought another couple of rocks from him and he left. My mind was somersaulting with crazy abstract thoughts bouncing around like a jack in the box. I then went into my bedroom lay across the bed my eyes wide open and drifted into my imagination – remembering a time in Thailand when my adult son first smoked crystal meth with me.

When the housemaid arrived, I was just lying on my bed – and I didn't get up. I just let her go about her duties. I hadn't slept at all, still in a fuzzy state of mind.

When she left, I got up from the bed and drank lots of water feeling dehydrated from the crystal meth session with Tim. My mind was now invaded with a kaleidoscope of not-so-colourful thoughts, at the forefront was that little girl. I was talking out loud to myself telling her to fuck off and leave me alone. It was now afternoon and I went downstairs the sunlight blinding me. I headed to the washroom and took a cold shower. I shaved my head and returned upstairs sat on my porch planning out a way to go back to Kep. The little girl appeared to be a pleasant companion at times if it wasn't for the fact, she kept nagging at me. I sat and chatted with her but was not at ease having that certain feeling, she was correct in reminding me of my mission.

I went into my room and put on my saffron attire tying the garrotte tightly around my waist. I then put the photo of the abuser into my wallet along with the mantra. Before leaving my house, which was now late afternoon decided to have another smoke of meth which I still had from Tim's visit. This time I used tin foil to chase the smoke into my lungs, as Tim had taken his pipe with him.

My intention was to go to the abuser's workplace before five that evening to lay in wait for him as he headed for home.

The road to Kep is not a busy one. I passed by the factory where he worked, drove on for a couple of miles, and stopped. I was going to put my motorbike into the middle of the road as if I had a breakdown. As it got nearer the time for the workers to finish, I waited for him to appear. A few motorbikes had come along and when a car came by, I just pushed the bike to the side of the road.

I did not have to wait too long until I saw his blue car approaching. My motorbike engine was still running spreading out my arms indicating that he stopped, which he did. On my approach to his car, my heart thumping, having already gripped my garrotte firmly in my hand out of sight.

"Excuse me, mister," I mumbled incoherently waving one of my hands then went to the back door of his car and opened it. I could see through the windscreen by the expression on his face he was surprised or confused. As if I had been asking him to give me a lift. I hadn't gotten fully onto the back when I wrapped the garrotte around his neck and then pulled him back against his seat.

He managed to half turn his head to face me but the weight of his body had dropped him down making the garotte tighten more.

DIARY OF A SAFFRON ASSASSIN

As he struggled his face contorted, and his eyes bulged while his legs kicked at the dashboard and window screen.

I squeezed until his last gasp for air expelled from his lungs. It had taken a long time - it felt like an eternity before he stopped struggling. I looked into his face his lips were twisted and part of his tongue protruded with a white foam stuck to the side of his face. I wanted to stick the mantra up his abusing ass but hadn't prepared properly nor did I have the time. So, instead, I took the mantra and poked it into his ear, and then spat in his face. I hadn't taken notice that drivers on their motorcycles just drove around the parked car but another car had stopped behind him.

It was fortunate and luckily for me, the driver hadn't come out to see what the holdup was about. I kept my head down jumped back onto my motorbike and swerved passed the parked car heading back towards Kampot.

On the way back, a voice in my head was telling me *that was fucking stupid*, then the other voice that I was more familiar with but becoming less comfortable was saying *you are a very good man*.

I got home around 7pm. It was dark so I went upstairs lit an oil lamp and sat down in total exhaustion. My head was in fragments and I immediately picked up the foil and started to smoke some crystal which made me feel better. It only took seconds before my skin felt like it was melting. Sweat beads ran down my back and dripped from my forehead.

My little friend sat beside me, she was smiling and rested her head on my shoulder like a long-lost daughter returning home. The crystal meth had turned my ghost visions into a reality and now the spirit had become vivid and in my face. I could see the colours of her shabby dress and mud-stained feet, they were as clear as day. The lamplight was flickering my shadow on the wall beside me, but I noticed with interest that she had no shadow.

The seesawing conflict of my mind had me momentarily neurotic and then euphoric. My brain was in fast mode with the overload of crystal meth. There was a righteous side along with a destructive side which was leading to my damnation.

The voices in my head repeated, again and again, *you had better get yourself back into a retreat you are a fucking lunatic.* The other voice was saying *you are a good man.* I was demented my jaw ached, my skin crawled, and I went to lay on my bed writhing like a snake shedding its skin until morning.

The next day, I just sat around my house all day wrestling the demons from my mind and reliving the incident of how stupid I had acted by killing the child abuser in broad daylight. Then I heard a call coming from Richard's house and got up and waved my hand indicating for him to come to my place.

Richard seemed eager to tell me the local news, he hadn't sat down before he excitedly said, "Did you hear about the murder in Kep?"

I felt his words explode in my heart; my mind was screaming this is a warning sign.

Richard went into detail about witnesses who reportedly said that he had been killed by someone in an orange suit riding a black motorbike.

Fuck me, it seemed Richard was looking straight through me knowing he had seen me wearing my orange attire often enough and he certainly knew the colour of my motorbike. The police will soon be onto me being easily recognizable, especially being a foreigner in a monk outfit. The paranoia was running out of me and my mind was still fogged up from the crystal meth. I had a headache and excused myself saying to Richard I didn't sleep well last night, making up a story telling him I had diarrhoea.

I felt relieved once he had departed, then went and took a cold shower, returned to my room, and lay down again breathing deeply through my nose hoping that my mind would clear.

It was not very long after, that Duka and Roza arrived with an inquisitive look in their eyes. They immediately asked if I had heard the news about the killing in Kep.

I replied, "No," and didn't mention Richard visiting me.

They both looked at each other with confused expressions on their faces. Duka said, "We just spoke to Richard and we discussed that incident in Kep, he told us he had just visited you didn't he mention it?"

The look on my face must have spoken volumes.

Roza said, "What is going on with you? Are you crazy?"

Exhaling loudly, I placed my hands over my face feeling exposed.

Duka said, "It is so obvious - someone in an orange suit driving a black motorbike? And Roza has already given you a photo of the bastard. We both immediately knew it was you."

I asked them, "Do you think anyone else would suspect it was me?"

They replied in unison that they did not know and we needed to talk it over.

I told them about my visit from Tim and the crystal meth session.

Duka said that explains your irrational behaviour.

We sat and went over every detail going back to my first visit to Kep. Eventually, Duka said, "Look, my friend, you cannot take all the abuse of these children personally. Roza and I are focusing on the organizations that traffic children on a larger scale. We have uncovered orphanages and adoption agencies that are doing this. We know we cannot bring them all to justice to face their crimes because they are supported by government officials and the police. It is about receiving money these people are being given - grants handed out by overseas charities - and some are also part of a larger paedophile ring."

I was deluded thinking that I was some sort of saviour, what Duka said made me realise that I might be a hindrance overall.

Without much more comment Roza and Duka went over to Bodhi Villa to eat and have a beer.

I stayed at my house brooding at my stupidity. Once again that night I was visited by the spirit of that little girl, with a beaming grin of approval on her sometimes demonic or angelic face. It depended on what action had taken place to satisfy her continuous pursuit of revenge.

DARK WEB IDEA

That weekend, Duka and Roza came to the house and I asked for any further news regarding the incident in Kep.

Roza said, "We haven't heard anything more."

Duka then explained to me an idea their friend had regarding a Japanese suicide help group. Duka said that his friend had contacted them on the dark web. His hacker friend in Moscow had the idea of recruiting them to take part in killing abusers before they took their own lives. I was in shock listening to his friend's suggestion and in deeper shock that Roza didn't reject the whole idea as ludicrous.

I said, "Are you fucking serious or what?"

Duka went on to explain that his friend in Moscow had been in touch with a self-help group in Tokyo. Going on he said, "Children in senior high school and university students suffered bullying on campus and pressure at home from parents and could not cope - thus resulting in them taking their own lives."

"What the fuck has that got to do with helping them by getting them to kill abusers?" I asked with a sickened frown on my face.

Duka continued, "The Japanese are very honourable people, I believe it would make them feel worthy if they did not end their lives feeling useless."

I sneered at him, "What the fuck are you, some psychological expert or what?"

"I am not but Roza has a deep insight into how to assess people's character when they feel worthless."

My head was shaking, my eyes rolling upwards, I just said to Duka, "My mind cannot take all this in, we can discuss it another day."

I rolled a fat marijuana joint saying let's just sit back and think this over, but my mind would not let it go.

"Fuck me," I said. "Japanese suicide children, where did that idea come from? "Watching a movie about kamikaze pilots bombing Pearl Harbor." I blew smoke at Duka with a puzzled bemused look on my face.

Roza intervened, "Actually you are not too far off the track." Roza went on to say, "That is where dying for an honourable cause comes into play. The Japanese hold great pride and honour in saving face, or maybe I should say not shaming their families."

"Wow! Hold on. What has taken their own lives got to do with honour?"

Roza continued, "It is such a complicated thought process to explain, all I can tell you is it is in their psyche. It is just an idea Duka and his friend have started to explore."

I passed the joint to Roza, she went into her bag handed me a few printed documents, and said, "Read this, we are going into town and will call back and visit you later tonight."

Duka took the remains of the joint with him and repeated what Roza had said, "Don't forget to read those documents!" Then they departed.

My mind hadn't resolved the Kep scenario yet, never mind thinking about Japanese suicide children. When they had gone, I sat down and read several articles that they had given me. It appeared all the same, just more and more stories about women and child abuse. Shocking, violent acts lacking in empathy or compassion for the victims who often were traumatized for life.

I lost my focus and concentration and didn't want to fill my already overactive mind with more horror stories. I had the sudden urge to get drunk to obliterate my mind in the hope of waking up in another life far from this abstract reality. I instead just lay on the floor of my porch looking at the now darkening sky closed my eyes trying to clear my mind.

.oOo.

It was Saturday night at the bar, Bodhi was full of young travellers having a good time sharing their stories of adventures around Cambodia. I sat with a few of them on the floor enjoying their tales of near-death experiences on the busy roads of some cities they had travelled through. One young lady who sat opposite me asked the group did anyone hear about the killing in Kep. I looked at the floor and kept silent.

One of the waiters at Bodhi said, "Yes it was just recently. But the police have someone in custody."

I pretended not to have heard about this new revelation, but my ears perked up. She began to tell her version of the story.

Her account was a man from a nearby village had problems with the murdered victim regarding being fired from his job. I was just about to get up and leave when Duka and Roza entered and they waved me over to join them at another table.

Duka immediately began telling me that his friend had made contact with some young Japanese people and that they were willing to come to Cambodia.

"Really?" an involuntary gasp spouted from my mouth.

Duka went on, "It has been arranged for us to meet someone in a couple of weeks in Sihanoukville."

Roza suggested that it should be me who meets with the girl.

"You want me to go and meet a young Japanese girl? Does she know what she will be doing when she gets here? And what has your friend discussed with her?"

We went over to my house and Roza took out a paper from her bag and read it to me as it was written in Russian. It was a clear and precise message that their friend in Moscow had connected with a group of young Japanese dark web users. Roza continued that they would be sending over a representative to Cambodia to meet up with our group.

I stopped her and inquired, "What group are we? I thought you were looking for war criminals and focused on wife and child abusers."

I was lost for words but managed to say to Roza, "This is all becoming too much for me to take in. If I am to meet this girl in Sihanoukville, it is not a good idea for me to go alone." I insisted that Roza had experience dealing with people who have suffered extreme duress. So, she should go with me.

Roza replied that she would let me know nearer the time of the arranged meeting and it was left at that. Roza then handed me a piece of paper whilst telling me about this abuser living in Phenom Penh and asked me what did I think about giving him a visit? This was becoming too much for me - Duka's documents, then Japanese suicide children, and now someone in Phenom Penh.

After Duka and Roza left, my mind spiralled into the odd and unfathomable connection, since the encounter with the spirit after leaving the monastery. I was thinking about what Duka had said about me not taking things personally yet handing me another assignment.

I sat in the lotus position and slowly breathed in and out through my nostrils repeating inwardly goodbye to the child spirit.

I repeated it again and again, goodbye, my mission has been fulfilled. It didn't help in any way at all, as she had entered my soul and had taken up residence there.

.oOo.

Eventually that day had come to meet the Japanese girl she would be arriving in the afternoon. I phoned Don, asking him to meet me at Ana-internet, it wasn't something to look forward to and in the back of my mind I hoped this crazy idea wouldn't materialize but it already had.

A taxi stopped outside the internet shop and they got out. As it turned out there wasn't just one person, there were three of them - two girls and a boy. I noticed they only had a small hand-carry bag; it was obvious they were not planning on an extended vacation.

I greeted them with a nod of my head smiled then said, "Welcome to Cambodia."

They could speak in badly pronounced English and all had a downward look partly covering their faces. It was my guess their age was around 18 -20 years old. We sat down and drank coffee speaking in awkward tones not really knowing what to say. The whole thing was rather surreal.

I told them we would travel to Kampot to meet up with Roza, but they obviously didn't know what I was talking about.

They answered in unison, "Hai."

I phoned Roza telling her about our meeting and she said she would see me at my house that evening.

Don had arrived and sat down for a few minutes, then we all jumped into his Lexus and headed to Kampot. On the way to my house listening to their soft, overexcited, voices chatting, sounded strange to me.

That evening after sunset Roza arrived.

I was sitting by the river engaged in small talk with my visitors. I was still feeling awkward and hadn't even asked their names. I let Roza do the talking from then on, she seemed to be getting smiles and bonded quickly with the girls. The boy kept himself apart he looked gloomy and tight-lipped.

Roza asked Don to drive them to a guesthouse in town. That night Roza returned to my house alone, I was sleeping, but she woke me up and explained the visitors were settled in. I told her this is all very weird and she partly assured me not to worry they are doing this of their own free will. Roza explained the meaning of Hochigo to me explaining these young people have been neglected since childhood. This was partly due to their parents overworking often leaving them with family members, neighbours, or sometimes babysitters. Roza went into more detail saying they wandered around the streets and those three at the guesthouse had all been sexually abused either by a neighbour or babysitter.

Roza had told Duka she would be staying at my house that night, and he made his way over to join us. We sat chatting and smoking marijuana into the early hours of the morning with me trying to figure out the mindset of the new Japanese arrivals.

After the Japanese trio had been in Kampot for three days, Roza held a small gathering at my house giving them instructions about their mission in Cambodia.

I listened to her explain to them in very slow English nodding her head systematically to each in turn to get confirmation that they understood. Roza was calm with no expression on her face as she instructed them on how to commit murder. I had learned that the young Japanese people didn't know each other and had been united by the Moscow connection through the dark web. I wasn't always present when Roza spoke with them over the next couple of days, but she explained to me that the two girls wanted to stay together and the boy wanted to do it alone. Roza had an assignment for them and planned for it to be done at the weekend.

Don had returned to Kampot. He was going to be the driver taking them to the place of the abusers. The name and location were given to me on A4 paper along with a photocopy of a woman's face who worked at an orphanage office in Seim Reip which was around a six-hour drive depending on traffic. Don insisted that I accompany him telling Roza and me that he felt uncomfortable driving such a long distance with nobody to talk with. I had all the details in my hand given to me by Roza and agreed to go along.

We took off Friday afternoon, and it was nighttime when we arrived. It was just Don and I with the two girls the boy hadn't joined us.

Don paid for two rooms with twin beds, we all went outside and ate then returned to rest. I wrote out two Mantras that night to give to the girls in the morning, with an explanation of what to do after they committed their deed. Roza had already explained to Don and me that regardless of the outcome of their assignment they could not return to Kampot for fear of exposing our group.

The following morning, we had breakfast together and then headed to the orphanage and dropped the girls off. The girls had been instructed by Roza about not returning to Kampot and she told Don and me just to drop them off at the building. I had no idea what Roza had discussed with them after their assignment was fulfilled. I imagined they would be taking their own lives; going by what Duka had said from his correspondence in Moscow. It wasn't something I had thought about putting it far as possible out of my mind. I felt deeply disturbed yet in some way detached knowing that two young people were going to ruin their lives. It bothered my heart and worse still possibly they were going to end their lives.

LAUCHLAN CAMPBELL

.oOo.

I was lying in my bed when I received a phone call from Duka he asked me if I could go over to Bodhi villa and get onto the internet and he would text me a link to look at it.

I sat at the bar and opened the first link he had sent me. It read that a respected social worker Chanvatey Sok was found dead in her office this morning with her throat cut and two written Mantras placed one in each ear. Witnesses reported that her last appointment was with two young women who had inquired at the office desk that they wanted to speak with her. Later, another staff member went to the office and found her alone and dead on the floor. There was more information but that headline had knocked me for six. I had come down to earth that this taking of someone's life had happened. Somewhere in the recesses of my mind, I had hoped the girls would not follow through with the killing and return home to Japan. I hadn't come to terms with my actions and now was facing the guilt of involving others.

I opened the other link it read those two foreign tourists committed suicide in downtown Seim Reip, by jumping from a building with their hands bound together with cello tape. There was a blood-stained photocopy in their possession of the murdered Chanvatey Sok, police are investigating a possible connection. My head nearly hit the bar counter as I closed the laptop. It was sickening and I had taken part in this by dropping them off with Don. The idea to use people to be rid of child abusers had originally come from Dukas friend on the dark web. The reality of his suggestion hit home and it now was a burden on my soul. I knew that it was me who had started this killing spree in Battambang but never imagined were it could lead.

That evening Roza Duka and I sat and discussed that event.

Roza didn't seem fazed in any way and even commented, "It is a modern way of committing Hari Kiri. It's a way of honouring yourself or your family."

I was thinking to myself this doesn't sound like a woman who worked for the UN - she is cold-hearted. Her face was expressionless.

I asked Roza, "What do we do about the two girls?"

She replied, "We do nothing. We don't know them. Their Embassy will handle any arrangements required."

I mentioned to her some people will know that we have had contact with them surely, they will be inquisitive.

"Yes, you might be correct but if anyone asks, just tell them we met in town."

I wasn't convinced by her basic reply knowing that Richard had seen them at my house.

That night lying on top of the bed the little girl visited me again this time she held a blood-stained Japanese flag draped over her shoulder, a contented sneer on her face my hallucinations were becoming more vivid. I sat up and confronted her asking why she had that look of contentment on her face but she vanished it left me feeling that I had been used.

.oOo.

A few days later Duka came to my house and told me the killing had gone viral. I wasn't sure what that meant and he explained. Duka said he had received a message from his friend in Moscow that hundreds of people want to partake in killing sex offenders, and child abusers. I inquired how would people relate this to killing as being sex related.

Duka explained both girls had diaries in their possession written inside was the reason they committed this crime.

I said, "Surely the girl's notes would have been written in Japanese and only be in the possession of the police?"

Duka elaborated that before committing the killing they had shared their intention with friends on social media.

I pursued my line of questioning. "What you are telling me doesn't make any sense."

Duka went on to tell me that his friend in Moscow had been following the girl's social media posts and had them translated. It suddenly dawned on me that this friend had introduced the idea and I knew nothing about hacking people's accounts. I was just being used as a vessel to implement his uncanny mind.

We sat and discussed this new madness that was going on, he told me that the majority of people interested were Japanese and Korean but messages were coming in worldwide.

Duka continued to explain it is the internet there are groups from all around the world and information can be accessed in minutes.

I asked him where they got the information from in the first place?

Duka said, "From posts that people publish also the news channels and other sources, I will explain more later."

In the coming days, we all met at my house Duka had an idea, "We will have to further our reach to other countries and make revenge a worldwide phenomenon."

Fuck me, what's happening I just came to Cambodia to a meditation retreat and now I am entangled in a web of organised murder and madness. I felt resentment towards the spirit too, with its intoxicated feelings of anger and rage giving me a false sense of power. This intoxication became dangerous, and my feelings of resentment were growing and turning into hatred. I didn't want to further communicate with her but it was out of my control.

Roza kept looking behind me and then said, "I see your young friend is still with you."

"What young friend?" I asked.

"The little girl is the same girl who sometimes visits me with her other spirit companions."

I turned my head around but nothing was there to be seen.

Roza smiled and said to me, "I know sometimes she can be overwhelming."

Duka was sitting with a bemused look on his face, as Roza and I spoke. He wasn't part of this somewhat invisible person's conversation.

I asked Roza, "What are you talking about – your other spirit companions?"

She replied, "There are hundreds of them here, all around the country. They are sharing their afterlife experiences, and some have supernatural traits."

I did not want to listen anymore; I stood up and excused myself. I was wondering how Roza could be having visitations from the same spirit and more, as she had declared. My head was boiling and went into my room and lay down.

NED AND CHUCK

I went to Sihanoukville to spend a few days with Don as my daily life was getting over stressful. Especially as I was getting more frequent visits from my uninvited spirit accomplice.

I went shopping for materials to have cushion covers made for my porch chairs at the market in town. Later on, that day whilst at the beach, I saw a blind man tapping a tree branch on the sand and his dog had a string collar around its neck to carry a plastic bucket collecting money. The blind man beat on the drum with his free hand and thought to myself that's an interesting subject matter for a painting. It was abstract, seeing such a contrast on a white sand beach with palm trees rustling in the breeze. Alongside this image were holiday-making foreigners, vendors, and drug dealers. This coincided with a parade of part limbless victims of land mines, cluster bombs, and God knew what other atrocities. Most of them were victims of the Pol Pot regime.

I asked the young Khmer guy called Dai at Chaimoi Frog Shack if he could take a photo for me and also put money into the blind man's bucket. I didn't feel comfortable taking the photo myself it made me feel I was being intrusive with someone else's disability. So, after taking a couple of photos I handed Dai a one-dollar bill to put into the begging bowl carried by the dog. It wasn't a pleasant scene for me to sit around at certain times of the day and didn't feel comfortable to lay stretched out smoking pot while these souls limped or crawled by their faces twisted in unsettling misery.

The local bar owners had them moved off the beach at the busy tourist visiting times, and by sunset, they couldn't be seen at all. I returned to the Villa pleased with my day of shopping, plus having an art project to work on. Don came upstairs, I was standing looking into the yard of the house next door when he told me that he had met an old friend of mine from the past called Ned. I didn't remember someone called Ned and asked where he came from.

Don didn't know but said he sounded English and went on to say he knows you from Thailand. I couldn't put a face to the name of any English guy named Ned, whom I might have met over a decade ago.

Don went on to say we can go around to his place it is only five minutes' walk from the Villa so that's what we did. When we arrived at his bungalow upon seeing him laughed and shook his hand. Ned had been living in Asia mostly on beaches selling weed. I met him in Bangkok whilst staying at the PB guesthouse on Khaosan Road. The PB guesthouse was a place very well known for the Thai boxers who trained there. The owner Mr Lee accommodated them at his gym nearby. Ned was a tourist hunter and if you knew where to get a good supply of weed then you could live well anywhere you meet up with other travellers. Koh Chang was the best place and cheapest at that time to buy weed. Chang Mai or Chang Rai in northern Thailand. In the 1980s a kilo of weed was $100.

This was Ned's occupation; he was the domestic supplier, as opposed to myself at the time I met him being an international supplier. So we had been in the same trade with different customers.

We listened to Ned's story of how he had been put in jail in Thailand on a couple of occasions for short periods. Ned told me how the Police chief after receiving money from Ned forewarned him of the next upcoming bust. Ted had fled to Cambodia, which was over seven years back and he hadn't left Cambodia since. We sat drinking coffee made by his Vietnamese girlfriend. Ned was now 68 and looking every day of it, he constantly rolled joints and he spat and splattered coughing germs around us. It was around an hour later he introduced me to another guy called Chuck from the USA who had come in with a young Khmer girl by his side - she was around 20 and Chuck was 71. This raised our eyebrows.

Chuck didn't smoke but liked beer which he brought with him. Chuck told us his story of how he had been here at least a decade before the influx of foreign small business investors. Chuck went on to tell us it was he who had named Serendipity Beach here in Sihanoukville when he first arrived. I knew by instinct these guys would have a deep insight into how the place here operated on the darker side.

We all went over to a coffee shop bar and restaurant called Geckos run by a young French guy and his Vietnamese wife who was lovely. We ate some nice food and had a good day listening to their stories of past experiences and then we headed home.

On the way back Don asked, "What do you think about Chuck?"

I hadn't given it any thought but said, "She isn't underage and it is probably only economics. You know the situation well enough by now, your friend at Gordons café is similar she is being housed, fed, and clothed which is more than most young people here."

I had arranged to meet Ted at Victory Hill that evening. When getting to the location Ted was sitting outside one of the bars along with a couple of other foreigners whom he introduced and whose names I didn't note - not wanting any association with foreign drug dealers, after my China experience. I stayed for an hour or so talking with Ted and walked by the bars on my way to get a motorbike to take me back to Dons. There were plenty of women to rent some young and beautiful but not for me. Don was the man for that, he loved to play around which was normal behaviour for a healthy virile man.

The following day sitting drinking coffee and listening to Don tell me about the woman he had met last night, as usual, *she had a body to die for*, he enthused using his favourite quote.

"Where is she?" I asked him.

He told me he had stayed at a hotel in town for the night. Don was still in a sort of bubble after his first encounter with Asia and the availability of sexy women.

Don went on, "I was in five bars last night eating and drinking then ended up at a nightclub with two women and two motorbike drivers drinking pitchers of beer until 2.30 am this morning. Then I took this woman to a hotel, no joking Loc, she had a body to die for, and you know what, the hotel included, the whole night only cost me a total of £30. I can't believe that it is so cheap!" he laughed.

Don was certainly correct in his calculations, a good time could be got there and costs so little, but on reflection, I mused, cheap at the price as long as you didn't catch any sexually transmitted diseases which were rife around that part of the world.

I spent a couple of days with Don then returned to Kampot. I had hoped a few days in Sihanoukville would distance me from the spirit girl at my house and distract me from the recent events in Siem Reap. As it transpired meeting with Ted at Victory Hill just highlighted the corruption and abuse that surrounded me.

A DISPLAY TROPHY

As soon as I got home Duka phoned me letting me know his dark web friend had arranged another assignment. I recalled the boy was shy when he had first arrived with the two girls.

Akasuki always seemed emotionless never showing any expression on his face, whenever I met him. He had never inquired as to the whereabouts of the two girls and Roza had not appeared to venture anything.

Duka had phoned Don asking him if he could take Akasuki to a place called Battambang. It reminded me having visited the Chicken Shack and monastery when first arriving in Cambodia. I also had a vivid flash of Conrad and his last breath taken on Earth but quickly erased that from my mind. I didn't feel remorse for Conrad as I had witnessed first-hand his treatment of women. I was feeling guilt-ridden that all these killings of sex abusers carried a heavier burden. I could have never imagined that innocent young Japanese were also dying. It was bothering my soul and I was becoming desperate to distance myself from it all.

I wasn't going to travel with them but had decided to take another trip to Sihanoukville to visit my friends the monks at the temple there. I hadn't visited them during my last trip. I had been preoccupied with meeting Don and having photos taken at the beach. I had neglected my original mission of teaching English and helping orphans.

I arrived in Sihanoukville and went to Don's house as he had given me a set of keys during my last visit. I had called him before leaving Kampot he told me to just stay until his return. After putting my small bag down and changing my T-shirt I went back to see the guys at the Frog Shack. I was greeted by one of the staff who gave me a free marijuana shake thanking him then sat down facing the water. A couple of foreign guys handed me a joint and introduced themselves – they both came from Canada. I smoked some weed and ate a banana pancake. It felt good the tension and stress seemed to ooze out of me. After sitting for a few hours more travellers joined us, listening to their travel tales and laughing at their mishaps then headed back to the villa.

That night sitting watching TV at Don's house I heard a rattle on the gate and got up to investigate and two young ladies waved at me. I questioned them on what they wanted speaking slowly and using hand gestures.

One girl said, "Mr Don?" with a smile on her face. "Mr Don, tell Mr Don, Ary here."

I told them, "Mr Don is not here."

"We come inside, okay mister?"

On impulse, I opened the gate and both entered smiling.

It was difficult to communicate or should I say near impossible. Their English was limited to mostly words such as, "You like me, mister? Do you like my friend mister? Do you want to smoke mister?"

Then one girl produced some crystal meth, filling up the glass pipe and before long I was laying on the floor eyes open staring at the ceiling spaced out of my mind.

The ladies were now lying on Don's bed. A few hours later when I finally managed to get off the floor I went and told them to leave.

"Okay, mister," one held out her hand, "give me money mister?"

So, handed her $20, and thankfully they departed.

I walked around the house in a daze, wondering what the fuck had I done, yet again in a momentary lack of self-control found myself drained and delusional.

Don arrived at the Villa the following evening he looked exhausted.

"Loc," he said, "can you make me a coffee?"

Whilst in the kitchen I called to him, "How did things go in Battambang?"

Don replied, "Haven't you heard? Didn't Duka get in touch with you?"

"No, I didn't hear from any of them."

Don sat holding his coffee and let out a deep sigh, "Fuck me," he said, "That young guy went right over the top."

I sat open-mouthed as he explained the gory details.

"Loc he must have knocked the pervert unconscious then cut the guy's cock and balls off. You couldn't imagine what he done next, he threaded the amputated cock with a fishing line or some sort of wire then he hung himself. He placed the amputated cock around his neck like he had won a medal showing off his prize possession. The news said he had written a letter but the details of that were not published. It is all over the internet."

I asked Don how he knew all this he replied Duka had sent him a link. "I stopped at Ana Internet before coming here and read the story."

"What the fuck are you telling me? Are you serious?"

Don repeated, "It is true, that young guy must have been fucking possessed or enraged."

All I could do was sit in silence lost for words.

.oOo.

I didn't mention the visit from the girls and we both headed back to Kampot the following morning. Back home, I met up with Duka and asked why he hadn't sent me the link.

Duka said he knew Don would tell me since I was staying at his house. Roza appeared to be happy saying that it was a great contribution to our mission and certainly would get media attention. It got me thinking what a cold-blooded lot these new friends are, not a touch of sympathy for the young person losing his life. It was like a similar response as someone clicking LIKE on a Facebook post. Then on second thoughts I remembered what Roza had told me regarding the genocide trials. It must have had a gruesome effect on her mind listening and watching films of innocents being raped and murdered. There was no doubt in my mind she was a very caring woman and certainly would not tolerate abuse under any circumstance.

Roza said, "Things have spiralled very quickly beyond our reach."

I asked her to elaborate and it had transpired that the paedophile murder and assault rate showed at a worldwide high. Duka and his friend had been monitoring various websites since the first one had gone viral.

I thought to myself well at least we had contributed to a worthy cause.

Duka then mentioned there are so many posts asking to be part of the mission and that we should continue getting outsiders involved.

Don spoke up saying he would be willing to be useful when he visited Thailand.

Roza said that was a good idea and she would look into the abuses on her UN files and keep Don up to date. Multiple ideas were going around and it appeared we were all willing to stay involved.

I mentioned, "Not everyone who wants to be part of this abuser's hunt would be willing to kill themselves, and our participation could be exposed."

Roza said, "It doesn't all have to be done in Cambodia and the only communication would be via the dark web which is encrypted."

Having no idea what she meant I didn't enquire any further. I mentioned my plans to return to the UK in the next week or so wanting to try and arrange for funding for what was my original reason for coming to Cambodia and was reminding myself it was for meditation and not murder.

It turned into an evening where ideas, suggestions, and future possible plans were made to continue erasing child abuse. Roza told Don she would send him a message when she returned to her job. There was a woman in Sihanoukville and if he would be willing to visit her. Don let her know his involvement was assisting with transportation making himself clear that he wasn't prepared to kill this woman.

Roza replied that there was no need to kill her but it needed to be known she was selling girls into prostitution. Roza had already prepared a letter for the police which she would drop off anonymously after Don had reported back that he had confronted the woman. Duka would also contact his friend in Moscow to have it put on social media platforms.

Don had received a message the following week, with the address of the woman whom Roza had mentioned at my house.

It came along with photos of three girls and one photo of the low-life bitch who was exploiting them by having sold them into prostitution.

.oOo.

We all met up again at my house the day before my departure, Don told us the story - as it hadn't been published in the local newspaper.

Don had visited her house scouting out her surroundings. He had returned several times and discovered she lived with another woman. Don had a plan in mind and purchased motor oil in a can, gathered chicken feathers from the market, and had been collecting his excrement and put it into a plastic bag. One afternoon he followed her and she entered her house. Don knocked on her door carrying a large plastic bag and pushed her inside grabbing her by the throat and throwing her to the floor. Don was well prepared, he went on to tell us she had let out a scream, but he had quickly silenced her by punching her hard in the mouth, and then binding her with tape. As she writhed on the floor, he proceeded to pour the oil over her head, then scattered the feathers onto her, and finally put his couple of days old excrement all over her from head to foot. He then showed her the photos of the girls telling her this would happen again if she ever took any part in selling girls into prostitution. Don then departed spitting on her face before exiting the premises.

Duka said, "She will be able to recognise you."

Don replied, "That is possibly true. I only wore sunglasses to partially cover my face."

Roza said, "You are crazy but what you have done will certainly make her think before she sends other young girls into prostitution." Roza continued, "The fact there is no mention of it in the news or internet would indicate she understood your message clearly. Duka said that the bitch doesn't want to be publicly exposed so has remained silent about the attack. It was her choice to remain quiet, so as not to bring any suspicion on herself or her dastardly deeds."

For whatever reason, we all agreed to celebrate what Don had done and went over to Bodhi. I was thinking that I was becoming a sick bastard for revelling in such a nasty assault. That thought didn't dwell too long in my head when receiving a nudge of congratulated smiles from my spirit companion, she was elated.

Duka asked me how long did I plan to stay in the UK?

"I'm not sure," I said, telling him my objective was to raise money to open or renovate a school for the orphans at the railway carriages in Sihanoukville.

That night was one of rejoicing and giving each other moral support. Don was mostly the main topic that evening because he had used a method called 'tarred and feathered'. I explained this punishment to Roza and Duka. I told them about police informers, or sometimes rapists, and other deviant behaviour in the community. The neighbours would deal with the culprits this way, not involving any authorities. It was an extremely unpleasant punishment as it took a very long time to get your body clean again. That bitch in Sihanoukville would have to hide herself away until the stains disappeared. Not to mention the psychological scars.

I was already packed and prepared for my trip back home and had said my farewells to everyone that night.

THE NETWORK

The following morning, I headed by taxi to the airport and after a long journey arrived home in Scotland. I stayed at the house of my son Scott, feeling good to be in familiar surroundings. I would be well-fed with good company. It was an exhilarating feeling to be distanced from the Cambodian events. I still had that feeling that the spirit was present so assumed she had boarded the flight with me.

My son took my thoughts away asking, "Do you want to go visit anyone tonight?"

I answered, "No thanks."

Scott then told me your good pal Robert Mc Kay is on his way over to bring you some top-quality hashish. I replied how does he know I am back in Glasgow my son said I phoned him that was typical about Rab always had the best dope.

My mind and body craved rest and I just sat around the house for the first couple of days.

I ventured out one afternoon to visit my friend Paul at his shop. Paul was the guy who had sent me the newspaper clipping after my interview with the press in Sihanoukville and had also assisted me with money. Whilst sitting at the shop smoking good weed Pauls son Fadge arrived with his uncle Eddie. It was a good reunion and we had some good banter about past experiences.

I kept in touch with Duka his messages were coded with simple terminology. He was getting feedback from his Moscow friend so the meeting of minds continued over the Internet.

I mentioned in one of my replies that I had a friend from Scotland who travelled all over the world - his job was as an electrician.

Duka asked me if I would be prepared to contact him to ask if he would meet people in the country where he was working.

I told him that he was presently back at home and I planned to meet his father at the weekend. I also mentioned my meeting with Paul and told him Paul was the one who had supported my project on the renovation of a school in Sihanoukville. I told Duka what Paul had shown me on his phone about a paedophile hunter's group in Scotland – they were known to follow predators and post their faces on social media. I told him that I would inquire more and keep him updated.

Dukas's response was, "We appreciate all the help we can get."

.oOo.

Alphonse was a well-travelled young man plus he was a bit of a playboy. I had known his family from my youth. I phoned him and we met at a marketplace in Glasgow called the Barra's which I mentioned before when first meeting up with Don. I was more of a friend with Alphonse's father who had a bric-a-brac stall there. We had a lot in common and he sometimes put my paintings for sale on his stall. We sat at a coffee shop and he asked how my life in Cambodia was and inquired if I was still practicing Buddhism. Alphonse had read the newspaper article about me.

I told him the full story leaving out the encounter with the spirit girl. I trusted him knowing that he was also part of the group that set up groomers online. They would create a profile pretending to be girls and then expose the men who contacted them with provocative suggestions and offers of money if they met.

He enthusiastically said, "YES! That beat sitting in a monastery." Alphonse then slapped me on the back laughing. He went on to say, "Killing paedophiles, what a fantastic contribution to society!" with a smile on his face.

I inquired as to what was going on in his life at the moment.

"I am heading to Afghanistan next week for one month, then going out to the Middle East for three months."

I told him about the group of people whom I had met in Cambodia and asked him if he would like to get in touch with them as they are looking for new recruits to assist in hunting down paedophiles worldwide.

Alphonse without hesitation said, "Yes of course, what would be my involvement?"

"I am not sure yet but I could send them a message today and get more information." I then explained to him that the Japanese who came to Cambodia were contacted through a dark web operator in Moscow.

Alphonse was certainly intrigued saying, "Put me in touch before I go overseas – I would like to talk to these people."

I told him before we departed, "Don't mention our conversation to anyone else.

We parted ways and I wished him luck on his travels.

.oOo.

The following day I visited my friend Paul again he had asked me what I thought about the hunters' group.

"I haven't looked at their site yet," I replied.

I had also informed him about what happened in Cambodia and he was not surprised, saying it was about time those bastards got sorted out. Paul went on to say that I should contact the paedophile Hunters, "They are exposing and catching those fucking beasts red-handed who are grooming children online. The fucking police are letting them go free because they didn't have any physical interaction with them. This fucking country has gone to the dogs, especially with government and religious organizations, and child abusers getting away without any redress."

It brought back to mind the documents Duka had shown me in Cambodia regarding paedophile involvement at the highest levels of government.

After chatting for a few hours, I went into town to do some window shopping and get my head cleared after my emotional talk with Paul. It seemed to be at the forefront of many conversations, everywhere I went and whom I spoke with. paedophile exposure was still the flavour month. Then just to reconfirm my thoughts the little girl spirit stood beckoning me from a shopfront door. I looked into the shop window this time, and seeing her reflection, saw that she wore a tartan plaid dress with a ribbon in her hair. Fuck me how can she be here and transform herself to look like a local girl, as I hurried away from her reflection and didn't look back in fear, that she would be behind me. There was a twisted knot in my stomach and I felt like vomiting.

.oOo.

I was sitting in Paul's shop smoking weed one afternoon when a young friend of Paul's son, Jack, came into the shop. He had just been released from jail that morning and was looking for something to smoke. Paul obliged by giving him a couple of buds of good homegrown weed welcoming him back to the land of the living.

We sat and laughed at some of his jail escapades and shenanigans that went on during his incarceration.

Jack asked, "Do you remember that fucking beast who raped the young girl in the housing scheme in Castlemilk?"

I had no recollection of it but Paul did, "Yes what about him?" Paul inquired.

Well, he is getting out tomorrow. I saw him at the reception area this morning checking his property before release.

"That's interesting," Paul said, then asked Jack, "Do you fancy that we both go up to the jail tomorrow morning so that you can point him out to me?"

"Sure, no problem."

So, it was arranged that Paul would drive us both up there before going to open his shop. We continued to listen to the jail stories. I nearly choked on the joint when Jack was talking about the prison menu.

"What did you just say?" I asked, "Prison menu? Are you fucking serious?" It certainly was news to me that you could order your choice of meals a week in advance. What was going on it didn't sound like jail not as far as I could recall when I was last there in the 1970s. That revelation knocked me for six a fucking 'menu' in the jail - I was sure that wouldn't make the hard-working taxpayers happy.

That night I lay on the floor watching television with my son but my mind was someplace else. I went into my room and wrote out a mantra for what we were planning to do the next morning - keeping up with my ritual as I had done in Cambodia. I wanted to be ready if we caught this beast tomorrow morning and wanted people to know the Saffron Assassin was alive and well.

The following morning Paul, Jack, and I sat in the car, the jail gate opened, and out-trudged 11 guys. Jack pointed out the rapist and we followed him slowly, he had stopped and waited for a bus. Paul drove down the road behind him as the beast boarded the bus.

It was around twenty minutes later and he got off. Jack and I got out of the car and followed him keeping ourselves a short distance behind. When he entered a tenement building, we both rushed into the stairwell and battered the living daylights out of him.

Jack slashed his face with a Swiss army knife and repeatedly stabbed his head and groin. Whilst he lay bloodied and screaming, I stuck the Manta into a gaping wound in his freshly slashed cheek where I could see his exposed jawbone.

Jack and I got back into the car and we returned to the shop.

"Fucking well done lads," Paul said.

Jack was grinning saying through his gritted teeth, "Dirty fucking scumbag got his comeuppance."

I appeared to be calm but was actually shaking inside, not because of the attack but because the spirit girl was still with me in the car not giving me any peace of mind.

The following morning newspapers had the story, it wasn't a front-page cover but it mentioned the mantra.

Paul phoned me and told me to come to the shop he had read several social media blogs about the attack. I arrived in the afternoon and he showed me an article that mentioned killings in Cambodia with the Mantra connection.

"Wow!" I exclaimed! "How did they put that connection together so fast?"

Paul replied, "Social media stories spread like wildfire."

After reading the blog it was trying to imply the assaults and killings in Cambodia to the same person here, but it finished off by saying it was probably a copycat crime.

I sent the link to Duka for him and Roza to read. The next day he replied, "Get back here as soon as possible - your services are required." Duka went on to tell me that Roza was being overwhelmed with numerous reports about the abuses not only in Cambodia, but also Vietnam, and Thailand. Duka said his Moscow friend was getting lots of recruit requests.

I didn't have to give it much thought. It was about time my flight to Cambodia was booked.

JUNO AND HANA

Whilst still in Scotland, I spoke to Duka and he told me about an incident that had happened whilst I was away.

Two Japanese teenagers, Juno and his girlfriend, Hana, arrived in Sihanoukville their minds were filled with a dark purpose. They had received a proposition on the dark web to become the harbinger of justice by eliminating deviants from this world who preyed on innocent children. The dark web had offered them a chance to make a difference by killing a paedophile before ending their own lives.

Whilst sitting in a cafe drinking coffee their conversation was interrupted by the sound of footsteps approaching them. Turning around, they saw a man walking towards them.

He sat beside them introducing himself. "My name is Duka," and then he explained to them that he had been sent to meet them. "I am aware of your mission through the secretive online conversations on the dark web. I am part of the group here to offer my assistance or guidance in carrying out your mission here in Cambodia."

Roza hadn't asked Juno and Hana to come to Kampot but she did tell Duka that the couple would have their assignment within one week.

DIARY OF A SAFFRON ASSASSIN

Duka met with them each day, the line between fantasy and reality blurred for them both. They were consumed by their mission, propelled forward by a sense of moral obligation that overshadowed all doubts. They had told Duka that the children who had already suffered at the hands of these deviants would hopefully find solace in the next world knowing that their abusers would never harm another innocent soul again.

Juno and Hana were given the address of a child abuser by Duka who had decided to join them. They took a bus to their destination which was around a four-hour journey. As they walked hurriedly through the streets of Cheung Prey, that night their hearts pounding with determination. They knew tonight was their chance, to free the children from the clutches of the drunken monster father who had treated them as nothing more than playthings during his vile gambling affairs. As they approached the abuser's house, the darkness seemed to wrap around them like a cloak of secrecy. Duka remained at the house entrance as a backup in the event something went wrong. Juno carefully pushed open the creaky wooden door, revealing a scene of debauchery within. The air was heavy with the stench of cigarette smoke and alcohol, which clung to their nostrils and made their stomachs churn in disgust. The abuser lay sprawled on the floor, his body a portrait of drunken slumber. Hearts pounding in their chests Bottles and dirty glasses littered the room, evidence of his intoxicated state.

Hana, her small hand clasping onto Juno's, looked up with wide, determined eyes. "We have to be careful, Juno," she whispered, her voice filled with cautious hope.

Juno replied, his voice trembling with a mix of fear and determination, "I know."

Silently, their hearts beat in synchrony, they entered further into the house, a sliver of light pierced through the gaps in the boarded-up windows. Juno unsheathed the knife from around his waist and then with sudden force cut the throat of the drunken abusive father. They had left a written message, which Duka asked them to do. It simply said, *'Child abusers will be punished'*.

Juno and Hana had eliminated a chapter of darkness, which was unwillingly a burden put onto those innocent children. They exited the house without haste and then returned to their hotel mission completed. The little girl in the house had awoken at sunrise and seeing her drunken father laying in a pool of blood. In a panic she ran to the neighbour who then went to find the carnage left behind by the killer. Duka went on to tell me there was a sickening article in the newspaper. It had given the story of the little girl finding her younger brother dead in the opposite room. It gave the gruesome details he had died of strangulation and had been sexually assaulted.

Duka had read the article about the killing from the internet sent to him from Moscow but he already knew first-hand about the event there was no mention of anyone committing suicide. Duka's dark web friend when first contacting him had said the people he was sending were from a group in Japan who had intentions of taking their own lives.

Duka was overwhelmed by emotion reading about the horrific death of the child. Duka worried about the couple but was thankful Roza hadn't invited them to Kampot which could lead to the group's exposure.

A couple of days later Duka received further information from his hacker friend that the Japanese couple had been in a tragic hit-and-run car accident. The boy had died on the spot and the girl had been flown back to Japan.

The story was printed in the Japan Times newspaper but didn't have any details regarding what caused the accident or if the driver had been apprehended. The story also stated that the girl would never be able to walk or speak again the injuries were so severe resulting in permanent paralysis of her body and vocal cords. Duka was in shock he searched all the Cambodian online news but the only mention he could find was a short excerpt saying that a hit-and-run car had collided with two people on the road. All this tragic information I was receiving about these deaths was having a negative effect on my heart and soul. It didn't seem to equate young lives ending to eliminate sex offenders.

I thought wouldn't it be better to have them put into prison and for those young people to live? It was becoming too much for me to bear this burden. I went over everything that had transpired since my encounter with the spirit girl. I felt that she had developed a God complex. I had noticed a pattern of her power over me and her ability to influence my thoughts and actions. I thought about her part in these killings. I wished that I hadn't been possessed but couldn't find any solution to get rid of her. I sat on the floor and cried praying to the Lord of the universe that those young lives who had volunteered to come to Cambodia to escape their miserable existence at home wouldn't reincarnate into revengeful souls.

THE MIDDLE EAST

Alphonse returned after finishing his Afghanistan contract and now started another job in Iraq. His correspondence with Duka had been about keeping his eyes and ears open regarding child abuse. Whilst at work Alphonse uncovered the grooming of vulnerable girls and young women. This information he had got from a female worker who had told him about an article in the local newspaper. The article was about young people trapped in prostitution and pimped out by a religious elite.

Alphonse was the type of young man who lived on the edge sort of lifestyle even though he knew the risk of having sex with a married Muslim woman, his penis would at times replace his brain. As it transpired the woman that he had met and who had told him about the newspaper worked as a cleaner in the kitchen of the hotel he was renovating, and she was a widow. It was knowing she was widowed that had first intrigued him, thinking he might get the opportunity to see what was under her Burka.

It was his co-worker who had confirmed the story the widow had mentioned about a cleric from an important shrine. Alphonse pursued to have an intimate encounter with the widow and they had a fleeting affair.

One afternoon during their lunch break whilst lying in bed she revealed her secret to him. This cleric was the same one who had also sold her to his friends in a prostitution ring. The cleric had secretly filmed her having sex with one of his clients and then threatened her into shame, telling her that she would be ostracized if the footage was ever shown.

The widow also revealed to Alphonse another cleric who was conducting pleasure marriages with girls, she knew to be only twelve years of age. Alphonse was taken aback by the news that he was hearing. After making inquiries with some of the local workers under his supervision he discovered the legal age for marriage is eighteen, but with the consent of the father, it can be permitted at fifteen. One of his younger workers offered him new Information, that in marriage offices near the shrines, some clerics are offering pleasure marriages.

In a society like Iraq, where unmarried couples can't have sex a pleasure marriage allows a man to pay for a wife under Iraqi civil law, but they are illegal under government laws. Some clerics preached that they were allowed under Islamic law. Thus, goes on to say that they can be a source of income for divorcees or widows. In short, it was religious hypocrisy to allow women to sell their bodies. It was a classic catch-22 scenario playing out.

With this knowledge, Alphonse contacted Duka asking him what he thought of the information. Duka responded by saying he would look into the matter and then forwarded to him a blog he had seen on the internet. It was about disturbing allegations that some clerics were making money helping men who wanted sex with very young girls. An undercover reporter was introduced to a cleric who gave the shocking religious advice that pleasure marriage with a child is halal. "From nine years old foreplay and anal sex were permitted," the cleric said, "as long as the man avoids taking a young girl's virginity. It's up to you he told the undercover reporter how you want to do it; she's permitted to you. You're allowed to perform from behind, to do what you desire."

The article was clear paedophilia was rampant in Iraq and much of it was being organised by clerics. This information confirmed what the young worker had been telling him Alphonse-anger along with disgust put a bitter taste in his mouth.

Alphonse was beginning to form a plan of action and had decided that when his contract was finished, he would visit the agent at the Mosque.

LIVE STREAMING

The little girl was restless and giving me cold arrogant and contemptuous thoughts urging me to return to Cambodia. I thought why not, having met all of my family and connected with some friends Paul, Alphonse, and a few others. So, the following day I went to a travel agent and booked my flight back. I then went to Paul's shop and told him my plans and would be leaving next week.

Paul had already suggested that I contact the paedophile hunters' group but I had declined. He went on to tell me that they have a good track record of following child groomers. Paul then went on to say that the group does live streaming. I asked him to explain what that meant.

He told me that they follow the groomer and film him meeting underage girls or boys. Paul had the idea that we dress up as Police officers arriving at the scene. "We can pretend we are taking the suspect in for questioning."

I said, "And then what?"

"Let's think about it."

So, we sat back smoking weed and running ideas back and forth with each other.

Paul said, "Loc, I have something to tell you."

"What is that pal?" I said giving him a queried look.

"I have been diagnosed with cancer."

That took me by surprise and came as a shock announcement right out of the blue. I asked, "When?"

Paul continued, "Seven months now since it was detected."

It was devastating news, as Paul was only in his fifties and had one son and two daughters.

Paul said, "I want to get involved with tracking down and hurting those beast bastard child abusers, and at least do something good before dying with this fucked up cancer." Paul had already decided that he would monitor the next livestream. "Do you want me to pick you up?" he asked. He repeated his first suggestion that we could go as undercover cops pretending, we want to question the abuser. Paul had already made up his mind for both of us.

I asked, will this be filmed by this group, and if so, how can we go undetected?"

"We will wear balaclavas."

I said, "Undercover cops with balaclavas?"

"Yes, that's correct we are undercover and can't show our identity."

I just replied, "Sounds good to me," but did not believe it and left the shop stoned.

I had read a post on Facebook from a lady called Amanda, advising me about how to post on group pages and to be very careful about what I was writing.

Amanda explained every group is monitored and that she had been banned for certain comments that she had posted about underage sex encounters that well-known people in the public eye had committed.

I sent her a friend request on Messenger inquiring more about her post. Amanda accepted my friend request after looking at my profile. Amanda said that I had put a post about a book I am writing that mentions killing paedophiles. Then went on to say that is a very delicate subject due to the recent publication and accusations regarding a Royal family member. I told her my book was fictitious, but she said that didn't matter and sent me an attachment.

I read the files about the US Government, and British Governments also accusations of Royalty being involved with celebrities in Hollywood grooming child actors. She had published a post to her group on this subject, which was taken down, but not before hundreds of people had commented supporting her point of view. Amanda was banned from using the social media platform for one month thus resulting in the dismantling of her group. Her post read: *regardless of social status whether it be Government officials, Police establishments, or the common working man sexual castration by injection should be administered to all offenders.*

It sounded about right to me and recognised that she was kindred spirit the same as Roza, Duka, Don, and a few others who were now semi or full-time paedophile hunters. I thanked her for the information, took notice of her advice, and stopped posting any more updates on my book.

That night Amanda contacted me again asking if she could arrange a video call at the weekend to which I agreed. I had often read her posts which I found were a mixture of true crime and sexual connotations with a touch of humour and very naughty. I watched a podcast that she had suggested that I subscribe to and that she had been interviewed by them. I thought it was a great idea as it would give me insight into who I was going to meet on video call.

On Sunday afternoon, we connected and she appeared to be relaxed with a confident smile on her face. We talked about our daily lives and our families. Then I mentioned to her that I had watched her podcast interview and was taken aback to know she spent time in prison.

Amanda's smile broadened going on to say, "We have something in common we are both ex-criminals."

I changed the subject telling her more about the book I was writing she said it is a very interesting and delicate topic and that was the reason she wanted to talk on video instead of posting on Facebook which was being monitored.

I asked her, "Have you heard of the paedophile hunters' group?"

"Yes," she replied, "I follow all their live streams."

I asked her, "Are you free tomorrow I would like to discuss something privately with you?"

Amanda gave me her phone number saying to call her and we could meet at her house.

Then she asked me if I would be interested in doing a podcast with Liquid Bullet Productions.

I said I would think about it and would let her know when we met.

I met with Amanda the following Sunday as agreed and she was very outspoken. She directly asked me, "Are you involved with the assaults on sex offenders here in Glasgow?"

"Why would you ask me that?"

Amanda calculated, "Your posts on Facebook are from Cambodia and now assaults are happening here with the same distinguishing signature with Mantas being placed onto the offender's body." Amanda also said, "I read the article about you being a monk in Cambodia and I put two and two together. I didn't deny or confirm her question but I knew that she knew I was involved.

I then told her that a friend of mine was going to follow the next paedophile hunters livestream, and she replied she always followed them.

I don't just mean on the phone; I mean he is going to their location intending to harm the groomer.

That is interesting she smiled, and it was left at that.

.oOo.

My youngest son Lee had suggested that he return to Cambodia with me. I explained to him that my flight had been already confirmed, hoping to discourage him. I did not want him to know or get involved with what I was doing. That is not a problem he said, I can arrive a week later and we can meet up. I knew he would be determined to join me so didn't disagree. He told me that he planned to book his ticket soon. We both headed to Paul's shop.

Paul was talking to someone on the phone and we overheard him mention that he was going to severely damage a beast abuser soon.

After his call, I asked him, "What was all that about?"

My son interjected, "Who is the beast that you're talking about?"

Paul replied, "He wouldn't know until it was live streamed."

Then my son being quick on the uptake said, "Are you following it on your phone."

I was panicking and said, "Don't be silly of course not."

But he was determined and pursued the issue.

Paul looked at me with upturned eyes, my face wrinkled with a frown across my forehead. Paul said he had just received a call that the paedophile hunters were onto a groomer and that he was going to follow them.

My son immediately said, "I will go with you."

I conceded saying, "Okay let's do it."

Then we had to wait for Paul to let us know the next live stream. My son and I sat around the shop for a few hours with Paul going over his plan of action.

Paul phoned me a couple of days later and said it was on, I called my son to meet me at the shop. Paul drove and he and my son followed the live feed to a location just outside the city boundaries, to a place called Cumbernauld. Paul had brought the balaclavas and gloves.

My son was relaxed and uncannily calm, I felt a little bit on edge, and then we saw the group surrounding this guy outside on the main street. Paul and I immediately approached the small crowd that had gathered. Paul pulled out his wallet and flashed it at the group. My son stood by the car door, and within a couple of minutes, we held the groomer by the arms like it was an officially warranted arrest. The paedophile hunter's cameraman followed us but nobody tried to intervene. Paul then pushed the beast into the back seat beside Lee and we drove off.

Paul knew that area well and had already planned where he was going to take him. I mentioned to Paul on the way they have video footage of the car registration and will be able to identify the owner.

Paul said, "Don't worry about that, it isn't my car and it has been reported stolen fifteen minutes before leaving the shop."

It wasn't a long drive and we came to a stop outside a semi-demolished factory. My son pulled the offender out of the car door whilst the guy was shouting for help at the top of his voice.

We dragged him into the building and I took my mantra from my pocket having it at the ready to stick somewhere. Paul had placed a plastic bag over the head of the groomer to reduce the volume of his screaming protests.

All the while my son punched and kicked him then slashed his throat with an open barber-style razor. You could hear the moans and gurgling sounds of blood spurting from his throat.

Paul and my son let out a spiel of verbal abuse kicking and slashing his face and hands. We heard a car door close then into the building walked a woman dressed in a beautiful tight-fitting red satin dress headscarf and large framed sunglasses covering her face.

I immediately recognised it was Amanda but didn't acknowledge her. This mysterious lady then stood on the groomer's face pushing her high-heeled shoe into his eyes – then without saying a word she departed.

Paul and my son stood frozen on the spot. I didn't participate much in the beating but took down his trousers and finalized my ritual by taking the razor from my son and slashing another asshole on him, then pushing the Mantra deep into his bloody anus.

We left him there unconscious driving back to town my son was in his element, his eyes shone and a slight film of sweat gave the appearance that he had just finished a workout at the gym.

Once we got back to the shop, my son and Paul in unison said, "Who the fuck was that woman?"

Paul said, "God bless her, holy fucking shit she looked amazing."

My son quipped, "She looked like the superhero Scarlet Witch."

I was thinking the Saffron Assassin meets the Satin Seducer but kept those thoughts to myself with no intention of speaking about my meeting with her.

The following day, it was front-page news, the paper headline stated Child Sex Offender was found unconscious, battered, his face and body slashed, in a derelict building. The newspaper article wrote he was in hospital recovering from his wounds. The reporter also mentioned the Mantra being found in his rectum and referred back to a previous attack stating they may well be linked.

RECONNECTED

I received a phone call from Duka keeping me up to date about what was going on in Cambodia, and that they were looking forward to seeing me upon my return. I let him know my departure date and expected arrival time.

He also told me two more Japanese and one Korean student were coming and that I could meet them as they would arrive just one day before me.

I arrived in Cambodia, happy to be back hoping that my spirit companion would now return to her resting place and get completely out of my life.

Roza and Duka were waiting for me at my house eager to hear about my visit back to Scotland. I discussed the events that had taken place in the UK whilst there. I was quite taken aback by Duka's reminding me that this group had a larger agenda that needed to be addressed.

I was annoyed that he seemed to be undermining my friends' actions. I reminded him that regardless of the country we took care of getting retribution on child abusers - my country was equally as important. I then went on to remind him that all the Pol Pot war criminals whom you are supposedly after are mostly deceased or certainly infirm and wouldn't be able to be sent to trial.

Roza put the matter to rest by saying, "Our main focus ... here and now ... is to take retribution on the women and child abusers. That is why I secured the job with the NGO office." Roza asked about my son's arrival.

I told her he would be here next week. I also let them know about the serious assault he had inflicted on the paedophile in Glasgow.

We went over to Bodhi Villa and ate while Roza explained the details of the recruits. There were two Japanese and one Korean all males. Roza went on to say that there were four offenders lined up three men and a woman, living in Phnom Penh.

I could see she was agitated telling me that they operated as a group committing their heinous sexual abuses on underprivileged children. Roza had decided that because it was a group of offenders, she wanted the three new arrivals to work together. Roza asked me to contact Don to see if he was available to drive them to Phnom Penh before the weekend.

I returned to my house after eating and then phoned Don he had just arrived back from Thailand a couple of days ago. Don asked me about my stay back home and told him I would give the details when we next met. I asked him if he could visit me and take some recruits to Phnom Penh before the weekend to which he agreed.

I sat making several mantras and getting prepared for the upcoming attack. It would be happening possibly at the weekend or shortly after it. That night I got a phone call from Don telling me he was on his way to my house. Don arrived and we chatted about my visit back home and then about the new arrivals. Don had embraced his role and was eager to get any revenge on those *bastard beasts* as he called them.

I hadn't met with the new volunteers who were staying at a guest house in town but knew Roza would have already briefed them and they would also be fully aware of what they had volunteered for. Don and I went into town the following morning, we met up with Duka spending most of the day just talking about Don's adventures in Thailand and mine back in Scotland.

.oOo.

The following afternoon we picked up the guys and we took off on our way to Phnom Penh with the three soon-to-be assassins, sitting quietly in the back.

On the way Don and I talked about mental health issues, it was a very odd situation. We were five people sitting in a car three of them strangers and about to commit murder. It certainly was a surreal event to be happening - to say the least.

Don and I were complicit in this, yet the two of us discussed it like we were going out for a picnic. I knew one thing for certain my mental health issue had been lit up but didn't become aware of this until the ghost or spirit girl entered my life. I was still in partial denial even after all that had occurred with my willing participation.

Roza had located the house that the abusers used and had given Don the address, but he didn't know anything about that area. We knew that the four abusers would be meeting the following day but at what time we also had no idea. I remembered having Gavins's phone number and thought about calling him to give me directions. Then on second thoughts didn't want him to know I was in town, especially after our first meeting outcome where I had killed the policeman.

That night we ate excellent food thanks to the kindness of my good friend Don. We did have some small talk with our new assassins. I had visited Japan on several occasions and told them I had been at the Love Comes to Town concert BB King and U2 at the Tokyo Dome. I could see by their expressions they didn't seem to be impressed or possibly they didn't understand - or it might have been because they were of a different generation. I had also visited Korea on numerous occasions, but I only knew some names of the local food and how to greet someone when I met them.

I tested my use of their language by saying a couple of sentences, they all nodded with smiles on their faces, but nobody replied. Mostly we sat in uncomfortable silence.

Don had located the area through Google Maps. It was a tree-lined residential area most with gated fronts, and all detached residences.

Don said, "We can't sit in the car all day waiting as they might not arrive until evening." So, he went over to the house and returned saying nobody was at home. He suggested trying to force entry and lay in wait for them.

I nodded my head in agreement, and that plan was put into action. Don disappeared around the back and after ten minutes, he reappeared as he opened the house's front door and beckoned us to come inside.

The interior wasn't fully furnished. We located a few bedrooms, one in particular, which was obviously the sex room having sex toys and bondage paraphernalia lying on the bed and on the dressing table.

Don sat on the floor near the front entrance to the main door as a lookout. The others either sat on the floor or lay down in one of the rooms. I heard the car door open in the driveway and we all stayed out of sight. It was early afternoon when four adults and one young boy arrived at the house. As they entered Don and the three young men grabbed them holding their mouths shut and forcing them to lie on the floor. The woman put up the most resistance kicking her legs and wriggling her body to be free of the hold Don had on her but without success.

I took the little boy into another room and sat with him realising that we hadn't thought this out very well.

Don returned to the car and brought duct tape which he had used on the woman in Sihanoukville for sticking over their mouths.

The woman had started screaming the instant she was manhandled.

Don then bounds their arms and feet.

When they were finally fully immobilized, Don and I exited the house taking the boy with us and leaving the young men to do what they had come for.

I contacted Gavin once we reached the hotel explaining a little boy needed his help. Gavin asked me to bring him to the coffee shop, where we first met. I arrived to see Gavin already there. I didn't sit down and just handed the boy over without explanation.

Gavin inquired, "Who is this boy."

I didn't give any response other than shrug, my shoulders and then said, "He is a victim of sexual abuse." Then added, "Sorry but I have to go now my friend is waiting for me," and left Gavin bewildered.

Don and I returned to Kampot. On the drive back Don said, "Your friend Gavin will know that we are involved in this scenario, it will be all over the news."

I replied, "He doesn't know anything only that I asked him to take care of a little boy, and that is what his job is." I did think Gavin could put one and one together. I already knew that Roza had had been in touch with Gavin. This was due to the fact they both worked in the same field protecting children. I suspected that he knew more than he was letting on. All I could say to Don was, "Let's see what happens, it is too late now and I assume nobody saw us outside the house."

The following day Don returned to Sihanoukville, and Duka and Roza arrived at my house.

Duka had a twisted look on his somewhat ashen face and told me the gory details of what had befallen the four abusers. The bodies had been so severely mutilated that they were nearly unidentifiable. The intestines of the four abusers were cut out and used to bind them all together, their throats had been cut, their eyes gouged out and four mantas stuck on the wall above their dead bodies with their blood.

"Fuck me," I let out a shocked response. My voice came out like a cat squealing, "Crazy bastards."

Duka continued, "And the two Japanese guys were found dead, they had been dragged from the river Tonle Sap with their feet bound together. They had left their mobile phones on the embankment facing the Silver Pagoda."

That got me momentarily thinking about why they had chosen a place of Buddhist worship to end their life. The police had their messages translated and they had also videoed the killing sharing with friends and on social media. Duka told me that there was no mention of another one, who was Korean, at all.

I sat in my house after Roza and Duka left feeling shaken by the horrific details of the method of death the abusers suffered. Yet strangely I felt relaxed being temporarily disconnected from Duka and Roza and the madness that had ensued since first meeting them. It was nice to sit on my porch again in silence, smoking a joint, drinking tea, and embracing the beauty of my surroundings. I was just about to lie on my bed when the little girl once again disturbed my inner tranquillity. She was in a playful mood, obviously content with the outcome of the horrendous killings that transpired in Phnom Penh. I grudgingly returned her playful smile yet somehow there was an unsatisfied gesture in her hollow eyes.

IN THE NAME OF GOD

The information about abusers never seemed to end. The dark webmaster had contacted Duku about abuses going on in boarding schools in Indonesia. He included information along with the addresses of the schools. He also put attachments with newspaper clippings from the local press.

Duka had a mutual friend who lived in Central Java and that was why the webmaster had sent him this information. He suggested Duka pass it on to their friend with the idea of sending more young assassins to deal with this atrocious behaviour. It was obvious the police wouldn't take action - because of accepting bribes, which had also been indicated in the newspaper article. Duka's friend's name was Bogdan, which coincidently meant given by God. Duka forwarded the attachments to him.

Bogdan's girlfriend's name was Hurrem she spoke fluent English and was quite an unusual woman. This was because she had an open mind regarding intimate contact before marriage, especially her being Muslim and with a foreigner. This was frowned upon she was an outcast in her village and moved to the bigger city of Semarang to escape the gossip and to broaden her outlook on life. Hurrem taught English and it was she who had translated the newspaper attachments so that her boyfriend could understand about the abuses.

DIARY OF A SAFFRON ASSASSIN

It appeared some of those holier-than-thou clerics and teachers due to their prestigious high standing would be immune from prosecution. It was the newspaper article's reasoning behind this was not wanting to put a negative light on Islam.

Duka sat with Roza and me going over the translated article sent from Indonesia. Roza decided something should be done and asked Duka to request the webmaster to contact more volunteers to inquire if there was any in that region. The problem was it was happening in different cities in Indonesia. I asked about the logistics for such an assignment, after all, it was in Indonesia and none of us knew the landscape. Duka said his friend would hopefully help to coordinate and he would contact him again that day.

The following day Duka received another message from the hacker saying he couldn't locate any volunteers in Indonesia. Bogdan had also replied saying he could accommodate helping him in one city called Medan. Bogdan asked if Duka trusted his judgment, that Bogdan's girlfriend, would assist at the school she was working. Bogdan said there was abuse going on there also.

Roza asked our opinion and I agreed, due to the fact the girl was a local which would certainly help as it was in new territory. The arrangements had been confirmed and the new recruits all came from Japan and would arrive in Jakarta the following week - their flights had been paid from dark web funds.

There were two boys and two girls aged ranging from eighteen to twenty.

The flight arrived and Bogdan met them at the arrival gate and he then took the two girls to the bus terminal outside the airport and bought them tickets. He told them to get off at the terminal in Semarang, where they would be met by Hurrem. Bogdan then returned and took both boys and they all boarded a domestic flight to Medan. It was a two-and-a-half-hour flight before they arrived. Bogdan had booked them into a small guest house and himself into a different one with the intention of not being seen to be associated.

.oOo.

I found out from Duka, after the event what had transpired. Not only about the murders but also about what the assailants had shared with Bogdan.

Bogdan had asked Katsu and Chisuke why they were prepared to give their lives to remove one child abuser from the world. The two men looked at each other and then started talking about their life in Japan.

They'd had similar experiences growing up most of their young lives they had been left to their own untended. Both their parents worked long hours leaving them to fend for themselves from around the age of twelve. It was a lonely existence, only shared at times if some school friend would visit and play video games. When their parents came home at different times often tired and more often than not their fathers only came home after they had already gone to sleep.

Chisuke opened up and told his new friend what had happened to him. One Saturday morning a neighbour came to the house, Chisuke was still in bed and got up to answer the door.

Standing there was a local man named Juni wearing leather trousers and dressed in a punkish outfit he was known around the neighbourhood as being wild and unruly. Juni carried a bottle of sake rice wine, came in, and sat down. Then they started a game on the PlayStation, while Juni drank sake and smoked cigarettes.

The frustration began to overtake Juni because he couldn't win any games and punched Chisuke in the face and jumped on top of him. Juni held him in a crucifix position and forced his penis into his mouth. Chisuke was terrified as Juni put the lit cigarette on his upper thighs and burned his genitals.

Katsu was shocked at hearing this revelation and then asked did you tell your parents? No, I have never told anyone only you know about this. Then when my father got home drunk, he came to my room and beat me for smoking cigarettes. He found the butt of Junis' cigarette and blamed me for smoking.

"I am very sorry to hear of this," Katsu said.

Then Katsu opened up about his experience, his parents had a babysitter come round to the house whilst they attended a company gathering out of town. The girl who was taking care of him had invited her boyfriend to spend the night because Katsu's parents wouldn't be returning until the following day. As the evening progressed, the young couple began to get drunk and watch porn on their computer, Katsu went into his bedroom just to lie down. At some point in the night, the babysitter and her boyfriend came into his room and sexually abused him. They forced him to have anal sex, while the girl sucked on his limp penis. When he awoke, they were still lying asleep on his bed.

"What did you do Chisuke?"

"I got out of bed, slowly dressed, and left the house. I returned later in the afternoon when my parents got home. My mother asked me about the night before and did the babysitter take care of me by giving me food. I told them, yes, saying she left this morning not mentioning anything about the boyfriend or what had happened. Both boys had revealed their innermost secret and felt a sense of relief after sharing.

Bogdan knocked on their door their door that evening, he had a plan on how to catch the paedophile. The article in the newspapers naming this school The House of Horrors had been translated by his girlfriend before he left for Medan. The cleric of the English department had issued several apologies but did not admit to any abuse. The parents of the children protested outside of the school due to the fact he was not investigated nor suspended from his position.

Bogdan had decided the only way to get the cleric was early in the morning at Fajr prayer when there was still next to no daylight. He would purchase two razor-sharp knives the day before the intended assault and also rent a motorcycle. The execution would have to be very quick due to the fact other worshipers would be on the same route to the Mosque.

Two days later the plan was put into action, and the three of them on the motorcycle would drive to intercept the cleric. Bogdan went to their room and woke them up, he asked the boys how they were feeling.

It appeared by their calm demeanour they were eager and ready. The idea was to stop behind the abuser then both Japanese boys would grab him from the back and slit his throat. They had the knives secured and at the ready.

As the call for prayer came over from the mosque speakers, they followed him in the early morning light. There were several people on the same road but at a relatively safe distance from their intended target. Bogdan stopped the motorcycle directly behind the offender both boys jumped off and cut his throat several times. It took less than one minute then they got back onto the bike and sped off. There were a few worshippers who tried to block their route but Bogdan swerved around them and their escape was successful. Bogdan had already explained to the boys he was leaving after they had fulfilled the assignment. He dropped both off in town and wished them well as he departed. The young students both wrote farewell letters in Japanese pinning them to their chests.

Chisuke stood outside the main Mosque in town and cut the main artery on his arm then his jugular vein then fell to the ground dying. Katsu did the same outside of the boarding school entrance gate where the parents had protested.

Both boys were dead on arrival at the hospital. Their final letters were translated both stating the same message that anyone sexually abusing children should be castrated and rot in hell. It was on the news that same morning and the community was in shock, others were outraged pointing fingers at the women who protested accusing them of instigating this horrific attack.

The press had quickly updated the article about the cleric saying he was the same one they had recently reported about, regarding the abuse accusations against him. The headlining article proclaimed *God's will be done*.

.oOo.

The two girls had arrived in Semarang where Hurrem met them and booked a room at a Kost which was very inexpensive local-style accommodation. Their names were Hinata and Chiyo. Hurrem had also booked into the same place but in a separate room - not wanting to be seen as associating with them. Hareem, had called her boyfriend and reported back to him what had transpired with her two potential assailants. She confirmed she had met the two girls at the bus terminal.

Bogdan sent a detailed message to Duka telling him about the events with killing the abuser plus the conversation with the two boys in their room. I read the message and felt disgusted at what had happened whilst in the care of a babysitter.

Hurrem came up with a plan to lure the cleric by dressing the younger Japanese girl in an Islamic hijab style known as Jilboob fashion. This style was very controversial in Indonesia. It caused a lot of criticism from radical Muslims, but also a lot of acceptance from the celebrity and youth culture. The style was wearing the hijab along with a very tight-fitting top showing the full shape of the woman's breast along with skin-tight trousers revealing every curve on her body. The plan was for Hinata to visit the school as an overseas student from Japan and ask about the requirements of non-Muslims who want to revert to Islam.

On Monday morning, Hurrem went to the office of the Imam and told him about the Japanese student who wanted to revert to Islam and would it be convenient to make an appointment for her to meet him. The Imam asked for some details about the student such as can she speak Bahasa Indonesia?

Hurrem, she said, "No. Only English."

"What is her age?" he inquired.

"She is 15," Hurrem lied.

"How do you know her," was his final question.

Hurrem replied, "I don't know her but she was outside the school gate just now and asked me if I could introduce her to the school leader. I told her to wait and would inquire that is why I came to see you."

The Imam said, "Bring her to my office," which she complied with.

The cleric asked Hareem to sit down with the girl, and the first thing he told her was, "This school teaches only in Bahasa Indonesia and Arabic, can you speak Arabic?"

Hinata said she could only speak in English but she would be willing to learn. Hurrem observed that the Iman was giving a lustful eye over the girl's attire. He told Hurrem to go to her class and start her teaching and leave him alone with Hinata.

The cleric suggested to Hinata that she take private lessons and that he could teach her without any cost due to being a visitor to his country and still a student. Before she left, he mentioned please wear less tight-fitting clothes and they exchanged phone numbers. The imam said he would call her to arrange the first lesson soon. That evening Hinata gave the details to Hurrem who said let us wait and see what transpires. It was several days later when Hinata got a call from the cleric to visit him at the school. Hurrem told her to dress with a long skirt which she gave her to put on. When she returned from her meeting Hurrem asked what did he say? The cleric had offered to take her to visit Borobudur for a day outing. He had said he wanted to show the beauty of her surroundings and suggested meeting him at the school gate on the weekend Sunday morning.

Hurrem didn't know what to do about this invitation but she said you should go to meet him and to bring her friend. This was a spur-of-the-moment suggestion, without giving it any thought. Hurrem was in a flustered state of mind, having not been in a situation like this before. Hurrem had her thoughts about how to deal with the cleric which amounted to putting drugs into his food or drink. She had created a scenario in her imagination that the cleric would invite Hanata to eat someplace and that's when she could have the opportunity to put poison into his food.

Hurrem was thinking about where she could get the poison and hadn't given this idea any thought. Later on, that day Hurrem received a phone call from her boyfriend, telling her he was missing his sweetheart and what the two boys had done and told her that she should be careful. Hurrem replied she had seen the story on the news. Bogdan asked her do you have any plan on how the girls will commit their deed? She answered no I don't have. He told her to buy sharp knives just in case the abuser put up a fight, Hurrem was feeling the strain of having such a responsibility. That evening she went to the night market and purchased two knives. Hurrem didn't procure any poison but told the girls to go along and maybe she could find a solution on how to deal with the Imam at a later date.

LAUCHLAN CAMPBELL

On Sunday morning the Imam was surprised when he went to pick up Hinata outside the school, seeing her accompanied by another girl. Hinata's friend was dressed in a very short skirt with leggings going up high in her thighs. The cleric got out of his car asking, "Who is this you have brought with you?"

She told him, "It is my friend from school back home in Japan." There was disappointment across his face as he had an alternative motive in mind having booked a hotel room. They all got into the car and drove towards their destination. Hinata and Chiyo sat in the back of the car.

On the way there he stopped to purchase water from a shop and the girls spoke with each other saying we had better do something now before reaching our destination. They didn't have any plan of action. The cleric drove off, Hinata spoke to her friend pointing out that there was a barrier on the right side of the road. There was a sense of urgency in her voice on impulse Hinata in a panic took the knife from her bag and stuck it into the Imam's shoulder whilst Chiyo pulled his hair and cut his throat.

As they were both in the back seat it was difficult to control his struggles. The car came to a sudden stop, thrusting both girls' faces into the headrest. Chiyo repeatedly stabbed at any place she could, the abuser let out a gurgled scream as the blood spewed from his throat. Chiyo opened her door and went into the front trying to pull the driver to the passenger side. Hinata joined her pulling the cleric away from the driver's seat eventually Hinata was at the wheel. The blood was all over their clothes and the car interior as they sped along the road. Hinata drove the car erratically and then saw a sign depicting a steep ravine. She put her foot on the accelerator veered to her left and shot through the barrier dropping hundreds of feet over the edge. Several cars stopped as they looked on and could only see a burning wreck below them. The police and ambulance services arrived soon after, three bodies were pulled from the wreckage all dead.

It was on the television news channel that evening, they had reported the cause of death was a road accident. They would not know the truth until after autopsy reports had been verified.

Tears were rolling down Hurrem's face hearing the news. Hurrem phoned her boyfriend and told him about the incident. She sat in her room and cried until she went to sleep.

.oOo.

Before the girls had committed themselves to their assignment, Hurrem had passed on the information to them that she had gotten from her boyfriend. Bogdan said that the girls should write something down explaining why they had committed this crime. Hinata had sent her confession the morning of the intended killing to a school friend on Facebook Messenger.

Chiyo did the same sending her final communication with the world to a Facebook group. Hinata's post added the screenshot attachment from the newspaper regarding the protests from parents stating the abuses which had been going on for a long period but were ignored by the police and Islamic higher hierarchy. There was a two-edged sword effect going on, the radical Islamic groups protested and often clashed with parents stating that those protesters were bringing false accusations and shame to the teachings in the Holy Koran. This was true in part but not all clerics followed those teachings from the Prophet.

The newspapers, several days later along with the television news channels headlined two stories. The first one is about the Japanese students and Iman's cause of death.

It stated the medical facts that the Imam's cause of death was having multiple stab wounds on his neck and head and his throat cut before the crash. It also exposed his paedophile behaviour once more that had been previously published.

The second story was about a Frenchman who killed himself in his prison cell after being charged with the sexual abuse of over 300 children.

Protesters stood outside of the government buildings across the city, disgruntled parents holding banners shouting and demanding a new Fatwa be immediately passed into law. It appeared the cycle of abuse would never address facts about Islamic scholars committing abuses. The stories about foreign devils infiltrating Christian establishments on this front all parents stood united. The parents demanded immediate action but it appeared government policy would always stand second in the eyes of the Muftis who had the responsibility and authority to change the law. The real power lay in the hands of those supposed holy men. There were more protests outside of the school grounds across the country. It had been ongoing now for several days, the continuing claims of abuse to their children, and parents were calling out for action and changing the system. It was about rooting out degenerate teachers and how the school had been treating their students. It had happened before numerous complaints had been lodged over the years, but up until now, nothing had been redressed. The protesters also highlighted other points in Islamic teachings. Fatwa is a ruling on a point of Islamic law given by a recognised authority.

The conflict between the government and Islamic scholars regarding the age of marriage had been ongoing for decades. The legal age from the government standpoint was 19 but if consented to by both parents, it could be 16, Sharia law is Islam's legal system based on the Quaran and the rulings of Islamic scholars. The Personal Status Law of Muslims 1991 allows girls at the age of puberty 10 years old can be married by judicial authorization.

"Nikah mut'ah" allows men to marry women for a predetermined period, have intimate relations with them then leave without any consequences. It is also known as a legal loophole for prostitution. So there lay some of the reasons why a Fatwa ruling or interpretation of it was just so controversial. It is in actuality null and void depending on which Islamic legal scholar is passing the judgment in Islamic courts. I could understand it was hypocrisy on many levels. In these modern times teenagers had access to the internet and what was happening around the world was making them think more about the double standards and restrictions of their faith depending in which country you lived.

RIVER BOY

Richard came to my house for a cup of tea and a chat, he was telling me about the Christian missionaries who were settling into the town. He told me they were from Korea and planned to build a church. I raised my eyebrows and said, "It isn't those Moonies using the derogatory term for the founder of the Unification Church the Reverend Sun Myung Moon in Asia?"

He gave me a tight-lipped smile and said, "No not at all. Richard came from a Christian missionary family and his father had done missionary work overseas.

I changed the subject and asked about his computer class progress to which he said he was thinking of closing his shop down.

"Why is that?"

Richard said the students don't have much interest and they didn't find it useful as there are no jobs that require computer skills available in Kampot.

I said, "They can go to a bigger city."

Richard replied, "What if they do not have any family living in a city, and they do not have the money to rent a place?"

I left it at that.

Looking out towards the river a small canoe-like boat pulled into my place.

"Do you know them?"

Richard stood up and said, "No I have never seen them before."

We both went down to the waterfront to inquire. A little boy lay across the boat in an inviting provocative position exposing his genitals.

Richard could speak some Khmer and ask them, "What are you doing here?"

The other person on the boat was a man in his forties who replied, "Are you looking for a boy?"

Richard replied in his soft-spoken voice that made him red-faced.

"What did he want?" I asked as they paddled away.

I repeated, "What was that about?"

"Didn't you notice the little boy?" he said. "The man was asking if we want to buy sex with that boy."

"What the fuck," I said, enraged. "You should have punched that bastard in the face."

Richard looked at me as if I was an uncivilized savage. "Listen Loc, you will have to come to terms with how the society works here or you will spend all your days punching people."

In my head, I wasn't thinking of punching people, but it was more like fucking murdering them, but bit my tongue - some thoughts are better kept to oneself.

Richard began to return to his house but I stopped him and began to inquire more as to what he had said regarding how the society works there.

Richard seemed to be oblivious to his surroundings. He went on to explain to me saying, "You have been in Sihanoukville you must have noticed the scene there, crystal meth and young girls forced into selling their bodies."

I could not argue with him about that.

Then he went on to tell me about the foreign invasion. "Surely you must have noticed, Western men coming here looking for underage girls. It is common knowledge," he spat out, "that the police are corrupt, the government is the same, and half of these so-called charities are not any better."

I was wrong about Richard being oblivious to his surroundings he was just overwhelmed and must have felt sickened. I know that I felt enraged when learning the riverboat boy was for sale. It was nothing new to Richard but for them to come to my house had angered him. He looked defeated and had acquired an emotional barrier for him to continue to live and work here. There was a clear downward look in his saddened eyes.

I walked upstairs to my porch in a silent rage of disgust. I sat down then it came back to me about a dream I had the night before - the little girl with the boy soaked in water. Then thought was there some subliminal message being given to me? Whilst sitting there and remembering that dream. I was thinking could it have been her message to me coming in a dream state?

I was restless, and not able to digest what was going on whether it be in a dream or what had just happened at the river.

It occurred to me these people were selling children for sex without any remorse or thought about the consequences. It made it seem justified that what the Saffron Assassin and the group were doing was much needed by reducing the number of predators in the community. I got this uncanny sense that justice was being done.

I made myself a pot of tea and rolled a fat joint, trying to reassure myself my thought process was correct and to blow the cobwebs from my mind.

THE KEFFIYEH (ARABIC HEADDRESS)

Alphonse contacted me once he got home and told me about what had transpired on his trip. It was quite a tale.

.oOo.

Alphonse was partly dressed in local traditional garb having a Keffiyeh wrapped around his head helping to cover up his features. He had decided to make a move by going to the Mosque with the pretence that he wanted sex with a juvenile. He knew this was acceptable under Sharia law according to the Nawal Al-Maghafi report that he had read. Some clerics were making money helping men who wanted sex with very young girls. Alphonse had brought one of his workers with him to do the interpretation if required. As it happened the cleric could speak English. The over-enthusiastic cleric was rather impressed having a foreign national require his services.

"What can I do for you?" the cleric asked.

In response, Alphonse said, "I would like a young girl brought to my hotel room on Tuesday of next week, how much are your fees?"

The cleric asked, "How old do you want the girl to be?"

Without hesitation, Alphonse replied, "12, and she must be a virgin."

The supposed holy man smiled, "Of course mister, but you know you cannot have vaginal sex with her only anal."

Alphonse nodded his head in affirmation.

The cleric then said, "That will cost $500," then asked, "What is the hotel name and room number?"

Alphonse had booked two rooms in advance for the following Tuesday one using the identity of one of his coworkers from Turkey and the other in his name. They exchanged phone numbers and departed ways.

Alphonse had a flight returning to the UK the following Wednesday. With the assistance of his worker, he had secured a batch of arsenic poison. He intended to put it into the food or drink of the cleric when he delivered the girl.

The day had arrived for the meeting, Alphonse had got room service to bring a large selection of food plus he had acquired a bottle of whiskey during one of his visits to Mosul. According to Islamic law, alcohol was forbidden but it was readily available at the right price and many Muslims took to drinking it secretly. It was early evening when Alphonse answered his phone and told the cleric to come up to his room.

The cleric appeared at the door holding the hand of a young girl wearing a hijab and a long dress down to her ankles. "Can I enter?" the cleric asked.

"Yes, of course."

Once inside the room, Alphonse closed and locked the door. Alphonse poured him a large glass of Scottish whiskey with ice.

The cleric's face had a beaming smile as he sat and ate the food and drank whiskey to what he thought would be until his heart's content. Most of the food on the table had been laced with the poison and the cleric ate greedily. He was a fat obese-looking man. The young girl sat on the bed not speaking with her head bowed. It only took a short time before the cleric started to sweat profusely and then gripped his stomach in pain as the arsenic had taken effect. The cleric rushed to the bathroom and started to vomit.

Alphonse knew he wouldn't be returning and let him lay there moaning and vomiting. knowing he would soon be dead.

After an hour or more Alphonse went into the bathroom looked down at the now motionless cleric then collected the food and flushed it all down the toilet. He picked up the whiskey bottle and took the girl who hadn't spoken nor moved from the bed since her arrival.

Alphonse then took the girl to the other room; he had booked under his name. That night Alphonse didn't sleep. He watched over the little girl until the sun rose, then gathered his luggage.

Before leaving, he returned to the first room looked into the toilet and could smell the strong odour from the vomiting and death. He made sure he didn't leave any fingerprints or traces of him being there then proceeded to the breakfast area of the hotel with his bags and the little girl. It was a buffet-style breakfast and the girl ate heartily she had never seen such an abundance of food.

Alphonse left her at the table knowing some staff member would approach her when the breakfast buffet was to be cleared. He went outside and boarded a taxi to the airport sitting back and feeling pleased that he had rid the world of a monster. The flight took off, and he began to think about the possibility of cameras in the hotel lobby that might identify him.

Alphonse knew he had checked in under two names and the body would not be found in his room and didn't give it any more thought. His main concern was that the little girl would be safe and returned to her family.

LAUCHLAN CAMPBELL

.oOo.

Once Alphonse had got home, he let me know the details of what had happened at the hotel. I replied that I would pass on the information to Duka, and I thanked him for his contribution to bringing justice to a worthy cause.

That evening I spoke with Duka and gave him the details. He said he would contact his friend in Moscow. A couple of days later Duka and Roza visited me with the news that the death of the cleric had been published. Roza asked me to thank my friend and then said we have something to discuss with you regarding press releases.

There was an article in the national newspaper referring to the recent killings and assaults that all had happened within a short period of time. The main focus of the article was the mantras and foreign suicides. The reporter conjectured that he believed all this was linked to some group or a serial killer living in Cambodia. The deaths in Indonesia although similar if not the same had him baffled though.

I read the article and thought he was certainly on the right track. The reporter had contacted the Japanese and Korean Embassies and had even mentioned the website for youths with home and school difficulties, linking it to a blog regarding killing themselves with honour. Duka suggested that we go to town as they had planned to have a drink at the Irish bar. I joined them and we discussed the newspaper article and they both agreed the journalist was very close to home. Whilst at the bar Roza mentioned that there was a scandal brewing in Kep - the place where I had garrotted my third abuser. Roza told me that a group of mothers had been protesting outside the school saying that one of the teachers was acting with impunity by touching the girls in inappropriate places.

I offered to give him a visit but they said they would handle this one ourselves. That was a bit of a surprise to hear as up until now Duka dealt mostly with his contact in Moscow and Roza with exposing abuses here in Cambodia through her job as an NGO worker.

I inquired about the war crimes project they were telling me about when we first met. Roza said that has been put on hold, "Our focus is Southeast Asia and to take retribution on things that are happening now and not in the past."

Duka brought the subject back to the newspaper article, saying he would contact his friend in Moscow. Duka would suggest getting him to post something so that this newspaper reporter would be pointed in another direction to throw him off the scent in Cambodia.

I stayed at their house that night it was too dark for me to travel on my motorbike without street lights.

The following morning during breakfast, Roza had decided to issue the abuser in Kep a letter that would give him a warning, if he ever touched any girls in his classroom again, he would be imprisoned. She did not want to take physical revenge on him because during her investigation she had learned he didn't have sex with any of the girls. This letter she thought would be the end of the matter, hoping it would resolve the issue if not, then he could be revisited another day.

NOT PART OF THE PLAN

Duka had been shopping at the market in town when he saw a Korean volunteer, Dae Jung, walking around in a daze. Duka approached him and then phoned me asking me to come to his house. I arrived and was shocked to see him sitting with the Korean guy.

"We have a situation here," Duka said. From what he could understand this guy wanted to commit another murder and then return home. He had just disappeared after his involvement with the killings of the four abusers in Phnom Penn. He had roamed around the city, staying in guest houses, and, eventually, found his way back to Kampot, disorientated.

I had no idea what to do, say, or think, his English was limited so trying to communicate wasn't easy.

"I want to return to Korea but would like to help one more before going home," he said in broken English.

I reminded Duka that wasn't part of the plan.

"Yes," Duka answered, "you're correct. The original message that I received from Moscow stated he wanted to help kill any abuser and then end his life. What can we do if he has changed his mind?"

I was lost for words but said, "What if he returned home and talked about what happened here?"

It was decided that we have to get together with Roza and discuss this dilemma. The young guy had booked a room in town and sheepishly smiled as we departed.

As we walked around in town, Duka said there was one other sex abuser in Kep. I suggested we wait until Roza comes home on Friday as she had mentioned giving him a warning letter.

None of us had foreseen the young Korean coming back – it had not even crossed our minds until it happened. For whatever reason since the Phnom Penh incident, I had assumed he had drowned himself as the two Japanese had done and his recovered body hadn't been reported.

That Friday evening Roza and Duka visited my house we discussed the predicament. Roza suggested we should get him to confirm his ticket back to Korea, then we can discuss his final mission. Duka shook his head saying, that there is no way we can ever know what he says or does back in his own country.

The following day Duka took Dae Jung to the travel agent in town and booked his flight for the following week. Now that part of the problem was temporarily solved. I mentioned Dukas's idea to visit the school teacher in Kep. Roza brushed off the idea and showed me the identity of another abuser in Sihanoukville and asked if Don and I could take care of this. I asked what about this young guy, "Couldn't he do it?"

Roza said, "I think it is better if you and Don go there. Both of you know the area."

I didn't put up any more resistance to her request.

.oOo.

I phoned Don and let him know I would be arriving at his house sometime tomorrow. The abuser was a club owner and he sold crystal meth, as well as sexually abusing children and putting them into brothels.

I met up with Don at Gordon's café and ate an English breakfast although it was nearer lunchtime. I was telling him about the guy who was our intended next visit.

Don asked, "Do you have any means of finding out where we can locate him other than his club?"

Replying, "Yes." I had his house address given to me by Roza.

Don said, "Let's jump into the car and have a look."

So that's what we did. We then drove by his business premises but it was closed. Don suggested we return in the evening because we didn't have any idea what time he started or finished his work.

That evening we sat in the car observing his house, but nobody appeared. Don then suggested we return tomorrow morning early and continue our stakeout. We continued to do this for another day but we never set eyes on him.

Then the next evening he exited his house we planned to follow him on route to his club and hopefully find a quiet spot where we could attack him. As he walked towards the road he paused to cross over.

Don put his foot on the accelerator crashing into him throwing his body high into the air and with a sickening thud he lay on the road. Don then reversed over him and began jumping up and down in his seat like he wanted to crush all his bones. I got out of the car and stuck the Manta into his bloodstained shirt pocket then we sped off.

"What the fuck were you doing?" I exclaimed! "That wasn't the plan."

"Fuck the plan," Don repeated, "that fuckwit is surely dead, and if he isn't he will never walk again." Don's lack of anger management this time had eliminated another abuser. It was dangerous because his car number could have been noted by a passerby.

We stopped at the beach and sat in the car, both of us slightly high from the adrenaline rush.

I returned to Kampot the following day and said to Don before leaving, "What are you going to do about the car damage?"

"Don't worry about that," he said, "I am heading to Phnom Penh later and will have it repaired."

We shook hands and gave each other that job-well-done look.

On my way back to Kampot I was thinking that this was all becoming crazy. Don running over the guy wasn't planned properly and the possibility of being caught was high.

I went to Dukas's house and told him what had occurred. He also said that it was a stupid way to deal with it, but nothing could change what had already happened.

I mentioned that it was becoming too much for me to cope with, saying that I might return to a meditation retreat in the coming weeks.

Duka replied he understood, "I think Roza and I could use some time away from all this as well."

.oOo.

Duka had received a reply from his Moscow contact after he had sent him the information about the young Korean guy appearing back in Kampot. The Moscow hacker suggested that he return home to Korea and eliminate someone whom he had uncovered in the port city of Busan. Duka passed this information to Roza, and she then asked to meet at my house and brought Dae Jung to join us.

Duka suggested this idea to the young man and he accepted without hesitation.

The sexual predator in Korea was an American soldier frequenting the well-known red-light district of Busan. The American army had been based in South Korea since 1950 on the pretext of stopping the spread of communism. The Korean War lasted for three years eventually causing a divide between the North and South known as the 38 parallel lines. The North became a socialist-communist regime whereas the South became a democracy. The American troops required all the comforts of home and the areas surrounding the military bases were soon occupied with bars, clubs, massage parlors, and brothels. This had caused protests from the local community but very little or nothing was done to rectify it.

Duka had given Dae Jung a photocopy of the military base layout and one of the soldiers who was to be taken out of circulation.

It never stopped amazing me how this hacker could get information, but I knew very little about the internet and certainly, nothing about the dark web.

Dae Jung departed on the flight that had already been booked a few days in advance of us knowing about this new assignment. He arrived in Seoul, and upon returning to his parent's house was welcomed with tears of joy. Dae Jung hadn't left any message about his departure from home or his arrival but instead had just not returned home from university one day. His parents had reported him missing and discovered he had taken a flight to Cambodia. They had no further information and assumed he had left home due to his unstable mental state from the bullying he endured at university.

Dae Jung had always been a loner, not necessarily because he didn't like other people but more because he liked his inner thoughts and feelings. He had formulated a plan to video-record his last moments on Earth. He had a lady friend called Ha Joon who had just graduated and was a kindred spirit who enjoyed reading books and had also been bullied at university. Ha Joon was petite in stature, she had a very pretty face with long hair but due to her height, she was more of an outcast with the fashionable K-Pop boys and girls. When Dae Jung phoned her, she was surprised to hear his voice and happy to meet with him that evening.

They met at a coffee shop, and he told her about his adventure in Cambodia. Dae Jung did not reveal all the details not wanting to make her feel uncomfortable. Ha Joon had watched the news on television and social media about the deaths of students in Cambodia. Dae Jung could see the inquisitive look in her eyes and asked her what was on her mind.

Ha Joon asked him why he left Korea and did not tell her or his parents where he was going.

Whilst at the coffee shop Dae Jung opened up and revealed his true intentions telling her that he wanted to take revenge on the American soldiers for what they had been doing, turning his area into bars and brothels bringing shame to the people of Korea. The Korean Times newspaper always had some story about violence with drunken military personnel and at times rape of the women who frequented the bars. Dae Jung asked if she would be willing to join him in going to Busan.

Ha Joon looked at him wide-eyed and shocked by his revelation but with no questions as to why. Ha Joon replied she would ask her mother if she could spend the weekend visiting her friend. Ha Joon then had a sudden change of mind and decided to join him whether she got permission from her mother or not and confirmed his request to film it.

That Friday morning, they took the train to Busan and booked into a local guest house near the military base. Dae Jung suggested they follow the abuser even going into a bar or clubs that he frequented. That evening they stood outside the base entrance and watched as the soldiers went out for their evening's entertainment. They had been waiting for over one hour when Dae Jung recognized the army officer exiting the gate. They followed him as he entered the premises of a pool club. Dae Jung then proceeded to go inside but noticed immediately it was mostly girls and no Korean men he turned around and left.

Ha Joon questioned him, then she entered several minutes later sat on a bar stool, and ordered a Coca-Cola with ice with the hope she would be approached by the soldier. As time went by nothing happened. Ha Joon noticed the offender leaving so she sat for a while longer then went outside and they both returned to their guest house.

Dae Jung had lost his patience after spending another full day and night waiting but had not caught sight of the soldier. Ha Joon would be returning to Seoul the following morning. That afternoon he went to a print shop and had several copies of large lettering with slogans that emphasized what he wanted to say as that was part of his plan. He then proceeded to a mountaineering shop and purchased a pickaxe and two ski masks then returned to the guest house and told Ha Joon his plan of action. He explained to her again he wanted her to video-record the events that would take place.

Dae Jung had kept a diary whilst in Cambodia he had revealed his correspondence with the dark webmaster to Ha Joon. It was unknown if he would succeed with his plan regarding his assault on the soldier. Dae Jung explained to Ha Joon that if he was arrested once she got back home, she was to post the diary and video on social platforms using the VPN server he had set up on a burner phone that he had bought at a second-hand stall. He emphasized that once she had shared the video, she was to destroy the phone. Dae Jung didn't want to be identified so the IP address couldn't locate where the video post was sent from.

Before they went out that evening, he repeated those instructions to video record the confrontation with the abuser. Both of them returned to the gate entrance and waited. It was late evening now and sure enough the abuser appeared and headed towards the same bar. Dae Jung didn't hesitate and walked behind him and swung the pickaxe forcefully into the back of his head.

The soldier dropped to one knee.

Dae Jung pulled the pickaxe from his skull and struck again, he continued this action until the soldier lay bleeding and unconscious. He then took out the printed papers and held them above his head with one foot on the body as if he had just scaled a mountain and had planted his country's flag on the soldier beneath him. Ha Joon was filming the whole event. Several passersby were looking on in horror. The road was busy with passing traffic but no one tried to intervene.

Dae Jung sped off running and disappeared into the night.

Ha Joon turned around and walked in the opposite direction removing her face mask as she went.

Later that night after walking the streets in a state of shock Ha Joon appeared at the guest house. Dae Jung was lying on the floor crying, she went and knelt beside him cradling his head on her lap and stroking his hair. That night using the burner phone Dae Jung shared the video on every social media platform, and lastly to the dark webmaster. After he was satisfied, he spread his message he took out the SIM card and destroyed the burner phone.

Ha Joon was deeply traumatized having witnessed and filmed the full event. They had the comfort of each other to get them through that horrific event. They didn't sleep that night.

The early morning light along with the sound of passing traffic got the young couple to untangle from each other's arms. They showered, dressed then went to a coffee shop to eat breakfast. The morning sun seemed to shine rays of hope and accomplishment. The newspapers headlined the attack on the soldier, he had survived the assault but was in hospital.

When returning to the guesthouse they collected their sparse luggage and went to the train station. Both had been shy and unpopular at school but what they did on that fateful evening would forever change a part of the world order. Their true identities would never be known to the world, but Dae Jung and the mysterious girl would never be forgotten by us.

THE WORLDWIDE WEB

The internet exploded with new information posts, blogs, ideas, and suggestions. Fuck me what was being reported on the TV news was just a minuscule of what was on the worldwide web social media platforms. There were posts from remote islands I had never heard about.

The internet was instant and it was globally accessible. People had woken up, writing their praise, about the anonymous actions that Dae Jung had posted.

At the top of Dae Jung's list was the USA's intervention on foreign soil, the list was extensive. Deforestation, Global Warming, Wildlife extinction, Government corruption, religious bigotry, banking deception, Hedge funds robbing thousands of people and leaving them destitute and homeless, and many more.

The video posted by Dae Jung started a contagious chain of events leading to exasperated everyday humans taking matters into their own hands. They started destroying the property of big businesses, who had no regard for the well-being of the planet but only the selfish greed to accumulate money. It was a non-stop barrage and destruction of some of the places that Dae Jung had posted on social media.

It was my opinion that on his written posters he should have exposed other abuses going on in the so-called places of sanctuary.

Dae Jung hadn't taken his own life but those other unsung heroes from Japan and Korea gave up their lives highlighting abuse and sex trafficking under the guise of child care. I began to realise our group wasn't very well organised in fact we were just a bunch of vigilantes with good intentions.

.oOo.

I had been chatting with that lady in Scotland on the social media platform Messenger. She was inquiring again about the podcast we had discussed when I visited her back in the UK.

In one particular chat, Amanda mentioned she had read about the happenings in Cambodia and other countries. She went on to tell me about a message printed and displayed during the assault of an American soldier that she had seen on social media - but it had been taken down. She went on to explain that a young man from Korea Dae Jung had shown a list of atrocities and exploitations going on around the world. I knew Amanda was aware and that I was involved in the whole setup.

It was just unspoken since the time she had stomped on the face of the abuser along with Paul, my son, and I – when she arrived wearing a Satin dress. It was Amanda's way of telling me she was still available if needed.

I had been waiting on my son's arrival but he never showed. This put me into a panic, and I phoned my other son back in Glasgow.

My son informed me that his brother had a change of heart and decided not to catch the flight. I would have loved to have seen him, but I did feel a great pressure had been lifted from my shoulders. My son then went on to tell me about two newspaper stories that had hit the headlines. The first story was about someone he had known from school. His school friend had just been released from court on bail for sexually abusing his stepsister who was age thirteen. The mother was enraged and once her son got home that night she bludgeoned him to death with a hammer, as he slept. I was shocked by the mother's actions but after some thought concluded the little bastard deserved all he got.

The other story was about two grandparents who had murdered the paedophile who was trying to groom their granddaughter. They had lured him to meet under the bridge by the river Clyde making him believe it was the girl who was talking with him. The grandmother had got hold of mace spray, and a stun gun, whereas her husband was ready for an old-fashioned man-to-man thrashing by boxing his ears treatment. The grandmother had told the groomer the designated place and time to meet under a bridge.

As the paedophile was making his way to the other end of the bridge, the grandmother blinded him with the mace spray in her hand as he tried to pass her.

In shock, the beast ran and jumped over the fence onto the river bank.

The grandfather was in hot pursuit and went over after him as the predator fell onto the grass. The grandfather kicked him hard on the head, his wife joined in by pressing the stun gun on his neck watching him jerk by the effect of the weapon.

The grandfather got enraged taking the mace from his wife spraying his face while he tried to cover his eyes. The effect of the continuous prodding with the stun gun had left him motionless.

The grandfather kicked him so hard he rolled into the water and both of them just stood on the river bank and watched him drown looking on without a second thought of rescuing him or for what they had just done.

There were several passersby and someone must have phoned the police. It wasn't very long before they arrived on the scene. They dragged the man from the water but he was already lifeless.

The police took the old couple back to their headquarters they didn't have any idea if they were involved. They were questioned but did not comment. The grandparents were asked if they wanted to speak with a lawyer but declined and requested to talk with their son. They then were held in the custody cells for further inquiries.

The newspapers published the story about the murder on the river Clyde. It proceeded with a flood of comments going onto social media. This killing, for whatever reason, had brought to light other abuses that were going on behind closed doors. There were stories online about drunken husbands behaving recklessly, wife beatings, and verbal and emotional assaults. The majority of people supported these angry mothers' plight for safety in the home and the grandparent's actions for what they had done.

The newspaper stated that although the case was still under investigation, according to the law the couple could be charged with murder. In the housing area, the old couple lived in they were pillars in their community. They always offered a helping hand and often went out of their way to resolve neighbourhood and family disputes.

It now was clear that the Saffron Assassin had reached from Cambodia into the streets and houses across Britain and the rest of the world.

I revelled in the wonders of social media via the internet. The news of the old couple's arrest travelled like wildfire across the country. Reports were coming from every corner of the UK. It had triggered a latent anger in the psyche of the population. It was mostly women who began to take revenge for themselves and their children. They went onto the streets from shelters for the abused, also homeless people sleeping under bridges hit the pavements protesting that even though they had reported their assaults to the police, nothing much ever got done about it.

They got together with posters and banners standing outside of police stations, it was a wake-up call for the establishment to get their fingers out and deal with this domestic problem.

DON IN KOREA

Since Don had crushed the bones of the degenerate bar owner in Sihanoukville, he had returned to Pattaya for a change of scenery - and to stay out of sight after that incident. Whilst there, Roza had contacted him, and she was telling Duka and me about her phone call with him.

There was a Korean woman who had lost her daughter to suicide because of her school report and not passing her exams. Roza had asked Don if he could meet up with her.

Don had replied, asking Roza, "Why do you want me to meet someone whose daughter failed her exams?"

Roza told him she just mentioned this to him because she had a gut feeling it was more sinister.

Don said he had never visited Korea before and had no idea about the Country other than the YouTube video Gangnam Style.

Roza continued telling Duka and me that she had apologised for suggesting he visit Korea on such a whimsical thought.

I asked Roza, "Why would you request something like that? It is totally out of character."

Roza said, "The truth is that I was visited by the spirit girl in your house a couple of days ago whilst sitting in my office. It has happened a few times but I usually ignore her."

Duka got out of his chair saying, "I'm not part of this conversation," and went to the kitchen to make tea.

I said, "Listen Roza this is all still quite new for me but I do understand something supernatural is going on. Can we just drop the subject?"

Roza said, "I just wanted to mention that it was the spirit who had let me know the Korean girl had been abused, and it was not just about her exams." Roza asked the webmaster could he search the website about young people in Korea committing suicide. A few days later Don had a change of mind - curiosity had got the better of him. He called Roza and inquired further as to why she had mentioned for him to go to Korea. The story about someone failing their exam didn't seem right. Roza then told him about her feedback from the webmaster.

The following day Don received an email with a photo of a woman wearing an army uniform along with her phone number. Don noted she had a pretty face, her name was Ye Jun, he got the country code and text messaged her letting her know that he had been given her contact details from Roza.

Ye Jun replied, "Is it okay if I call you now?"

Don agreed and was pleasantly surprised when hearing her English, it was clear and easy to understand.

A couple of days later Don was on a flight somewhat excited, yet also apprehensive as to what lay ahead. After arrival, he took a taxi into town checked into the LOTTE hotel and sent her a message. Don suggested that they meet and she could introduce him to Korean cuisine.

Ye Jun replied that she would meet him at the lobby of the hotel at 7.30 pm that evening.

Don waited in the lobby and she arrived exactly on time. Looking her over thinking she was very pretty he introduced himself and they shook hands.

Ye Jun stopped a taxi outside the hotel telling the driver what restaurant to go to. She spoke fluently, her English a welcome change from his encounters in Thailand and Cambodia. Ye Jun suggested they eat Bulgogi going on to tell Don it is a marinated beef barbecue that you can cook yourself at the table.

Don smiled at her looking into her eyes a little too long, not hiding his obvious attraction. Once seated Don inquired as to why she contacted the group over such an issue about her daughter not passing her exams in school. Ye Jun explained that her daughter had left a letter before taking her life saying her teacher had been sexually abusing her. The tears filled her eyes.

Don handed her a napkin and then asked why didn't you tell this to Roza?

There was an uncomfortable silence at the table. Don reached out holding her hand and praised her for being so thoughtful about her daughter's memory. Don diverted the conversation praising her for choosing such an unusual way to dine and for how the food was cooked at the table, saying it was a wonderful new experience for him.

Ye Jun smiled hearing his approval.

Don asked, "What about your husband? Does he know what you have in mind?"

She told him she was currently going through a divorce going on to explain that her husband's family blamed her for not noticing signs of their daughter's behaviour.

"I am sorry to hear that," he said, then asked, "Do you have any plan in mind about how you want to go about getting your revenge?"

Ye Jun said the school will be going on a camp holiday next weekend and I plan to intercept him on his way.

Don inquired, "How did you know how to contact Roza?"

Ye Jun told him she was told by a friend about a website regarding children committing suicide. Ye Jun had looked on the site to see if her daughter had posted on it but she didn't find anything. "I then decided to post that my daughter had been sexually abused by her teacher." It was a few days later she received a message for her to contact an email address in Russia. "I didn't know what to think or do but made the decision to reply and was given Roza's contact details."

Don was satisfied with her explanation and asked, "Do you plan to hurt him?"

Ye Jun looked directly into Don's eyes and replied, "I want him dead and I need someone to distract him."

Don was thinking she sounded definite with her intentions. He said, "By the photo I received you had on an army uniform, have you had military training?"

"Yes," she replied.

He didn't pursue any further questions.

The meal was finished, and being the usual considerate host Don insisted on paying but Ye Jun had already taken her credit card from her purse and waved the waiter to the table. Don tried to insist but to no avail. They departed making arrangements to meet again the following evening.

Over the next few days, Don met up with Ye Jun most evenings and he often flirted with her. She seemed to enjoy the attention.

Ye Jun had information about the time of the school classroom going this weekend on the camping trip. The class was going by bus whereas the teacher would be driving his car. She planned to pretend she had broken down and hoped that he would stop to assist her.

"It certainly isn't a foolproof way to meet someone," she said. "He will be driving a grey Kia Sorento with a roof rack."

Don suggested that he go onto the road and flag him down hoping that he would be polite to stop for a foreigner.

Ye Jun replied that was a good idea so the plan was set.

Ye Jun arranged to pick Don up outside the hotel at 9 am on Saturday.

On the way, Don inquired about her method of getting revenge. The first time he had asked her she hadn't elaborated, but now she put her hand into the glove department and produced a handgun.

Don asked, "Is your pistol military-supplied?"

Ye Jun said, "Yes."

Don told her, "Then it will be traceable back to you."

Ye Jun responded by saying she bought it on the black market from an American soldier. The gun was a Korean military issue Daewoo K5 Standard sidearm.

Don didn't pick the pistol up but smiled at her saying, "You are one smart cookie."

"What does that mean she inquired?"

"It just means you are calculated and clever."

Ye Jun put her hand on Don's knee and thanked him for his compliment and support.

They had arrived at their destination and stopped a short distance before the entrance to the camp. Ye Jun had pulled onto the side of the road and they both got out and sat on the boot of the car and waited.

Don suggested that Ye Jun sit in the car just in case the teacher would recognise her. Don knew the car's make and colour, and eventually, after waiting thirty minutes, it appeared.

Don stepped onto the road and flagged it down. Then he approached the driver waving his hands to indicate he needed help.

DIARY OF A SAFFRON ASSASSIN

The teacher stopped and exited his car and walked behind the boot of the parked vehicle. He had just gotten there when Ye Jun stepped out and confronted him. The teacher with a shocked look in his eyes acknowledged who was standing beside him, then panic showed on his face and he began talking very quickly.

Don had no idea what was being said but could see the rage on Ye Jun's face and, without hesitation, she shot him six times her stance was firm and decisive.

Then they both got into the car and returned to the city.

On the way back Don remarked, "You are a cold-blooded killer."

Ye Jun replied, "My blood is running hot now that my daughter's abuser is dead." She sighed and said, "Her spirit will be released from the darkness now."

On the journey back Ye Jun asked Don if would he take her to his room and comfort her.

Don smiled and replied, "I have been wanting to comfort you since the first time we met, reaching over a stroking her thigh."

When they arrived at the hotel there was no other thought on their minds other than to embrace. Ye Jun immediately pushed Don against the wall and then began to loosen his belt and unzip his trousers. She was in a frenzy like someone who hadn't been able to release her pent-up frustrations for a while.

Don pulled up her skirt and both fell onto the bed and had hard uninhibited sex still nearly fully clothed. They then got naked and explored each other with a passion, both devouring each other orally until they lay panting in each other's arms.

After some more exploration of each other, they both got up and showered. Ye Jun was glowing, her eyes had a satisfying light in them, and Don was feeling the same.

Don said, "If you don't mind, I would like to extend my visit for another week."

"Yes, that would be great," Ye Jun still had a glow of contentment on her face telling him, "I can have three days leave of duty, we could visit Jeju Island."

Don was in his element smiling and replied, "You are someone special." They went out to eat that evening. Ye Jun took Don's hand walking down the street like two young lovers.

Ye Jun spent the night at the hotel and she translated the news about the killing, saying the police were investigating.

The news bulletin had finished moving on to another story which they both paid no attention to, as they sat together snuggling close.

Ye Jun had been given a five-day holiday it was a magical time they had spent together walking along the beach at sunset on that final week, a love story of a sort.

On their final night in Seoul, Don had ordered room service not wanting to share their time with anyone. The following afternoon Ye Jun drove Don to the airport and he departed with the promise to keep in touch.

SPIRITS REUNION

Roza and Duka's original reason for coming to Cambodia was to seek out war criminals in the Khmer Rouge. I remember it was one of the first conversations they had with me, but the subject was never again discussed after that.

Over the months that we had known each other so much had happened but it was Roza and Duka announcing they were pregnant that gave me the biggest shock. A bit of happy news amidst all the bad.

It was whilst sitting in the hospital having her monthly prenatal checkup that several spirits contacted Roza, bringing to her attention the trial of war criminals. Roza, being a lawyer in the past for the UN, still had many friends working there and access to their website. Roza phoned Duka telling him to meet at Blank Canvas that evening.

Duka arrived at my house before sunset telling me Roza wanted to have a meeting.

We sat smoking marijuana waiting for her arrival. It was after sundown and she arrived holding a printed paper in her hand. She sat down and read the article which had been brought to her attention whilst at the hospital.

The Extraordinary Chambers in the Courts of Cambodia are commonly known as the Cambodia Tribunal or Khmer Rouge

Tribunal. It was a court established to put on trial the senior leaders and the most responsible members of the Khmer Rouge for alleged violations of international law and serious crimes perpetrated during the Cambodian genocide. Although it was a national court, it was established as part of an agreement between the Royal Government of Cambodia and the United Nations.

Roza and Duka spent the night at my house, the spirit of the little girl hovered above. All through that night she, along with her spirit friends, surrounded my bed.

I got a clear and direct message that her murdering rapist and the killer of her parents was nearby.

I didn't sleep at all then got out of bed to sit on my veranda. I was only seated for a few minutes when Roza joined me.

I told Roza that I couldn't sleep and that I was being disturbed by numerous spirits.

"I know," she replied, "they surrounded my bed also." Roza went on to explain to me that those spirits wanted to avenge the horrific atrocities upon the killer of their friend. Roza told me that when she got to her work, she would call me if she found more details regarding this ongoing trial and the killer's whereabouts.

I received a phone call that afternoon and Roza gave me the address of an old man who could be responsible for the crimes. The spirit girl had a look on her face showing delight. Getting the news that this man could be her abuser. In my mind, I was thinking how could she possibly recognise him after so many years?

I took a shower shaved my head and prepared my robe and manta ready to kill this despicable man. I got onto my motorcycle; his house was on a pepper plantation not far from town. I arrived and there were many buildings dating from the colonial period, including the Governor's Mansion. The house where the abuser lived was easy to locate, he lived behind the mansion. I drove past the house onto a dirt road and then walked as I got closer; I could see an old man sitting shirtless behind the house in a wheelchair there was nobody else nearby. I could see he looked half asleep, his head drooped but as I approached his eyes met mine.

With every step I took towards him, I could feel the spirit girl getting more and more tense. Finally, she was going to have her revenge.

When I stepped out in front of him, the look on his face was like he was seeing a ghost – because he did see one. Down at my side I felt the little girl's hand curl around my pinkie finger. I looked down and the little girl stood by my side she had finally recognised and met her and her family's killer.

The sight of him was disgusting. His body was covered by a syphilis rash, his eyes were nearly blinded with scabs. His wheelchair was badly in need of repair and it was clear that he was not being cared for very well.

I didn't feel any sympathy for him but to my surprise, the spirit told me not to kill him. I sensed that she knew his body was racked with pain and she wanted to let him suffer a slow and agonizing death. At this point killing him would be a mercy.

So, without a word, the little girl and I turned and walked back the way we had come. Her hand still curled around my little finger.

I returned home with a different awareness running through me. It felt like I had been liberated. My tortured mind finally felt at peace once more.

As the days turned into weeks, I didn't see or hear from the spirit girl again. I took that to mean she had been appeased and her soul could finally move on to another realm.

A NEW BEGINNING

We all met at my house to celebrate Roza and her baby. She had given birth to a healthy baby girl and planned to return home to introduce her daughter to both her and Dukas's families.

She arrived beaming with pride and asked if I wanted to hold the child.

As I reached out and took the tiny baby into my arms, I immediately had this magnetic surge going through my body. As soon as my eyes looked at the baby, I recognised the attachment. It was the same feeling that occurred the first time I placed my feet on Cambodian soil - and the second time in the cave of skulls where the spirit of the little girl entered my soul.

I cradled her and then paced across the floor. I was talking to her in baby language making coo sounds and smiling down at her.

Roza had called her daughter Aisha which meant 'living, love, and prosperity'.

The baby seemed to be content in my arms. Her little hand reached out and gripped onto my pinkie finger touching the scar there from my childhood trauma and rubbing on it gently. My whole childhood flashed in front of my eyes, and I had to concentrate so as not to drop her.

DIARY OF A SAFFRON ASSASSIN

In that flash of recognition, I realised this was the reincarnation of the spirit girl. It was as clear as the sunsets in the evening. I instinctively knew Roza was also aware of this.

Little Aisha would have a second chance in this life and be brought up in a loving family. It brought tears to my eyes and warmed my heart to think all that fear, anger, and hatred had dissipated and would be replaced by love, respect, and kindness.

Roza had booked their flight home for the following month. I inquired as to how long they planned to stay.

Roza said, "At least one year."

Duka added, "We might just decide not to return as we need to plan for the future of our child."

That evening after everyone was gone, I sat thinking about my childhood and the abuse that I had endured in my family house and childcare homes. I needed to let go of those deep-rooted resentments. My effort to become a monk had failed miserably. I finally realised that I was running away from my past – and indeed had been running away my whole life, from one place to another. Although my thoughts of becoming a monk were admirable my actions didn't follow suit.

Aisha had been the messenger all along, making me come to my senses and change my ways. What I wanted wasn't to punish and seek revenge, it was to help and support other children.

I decided there and then to return to Sihanoukville and teach the children at the Temple.

That night I didn't sleep well thinking about my past actions and what would happen to me in my next reincarnation. I recalled reading about Tibetan people coming back as a dog. It was considered that dogs hanging around Buddhist temples were only one step from being reincarnated back to human form. I thought that I would more likely return as a cockroach and would be reincarnated numerous times before being given the privilege of coming back as man's best friend. But if that is what it took then that is what I would do. Finally I fell into a deep sleep.

.oOo.

I dreamt that my body died and I lay there was wrapped in an orange silk Buddhist robe. I could see my childhood days mostly full of fun along with the darker times when being in childcare. I met all my family members who had passed on before me. I saw the faces of the people whom I helped and those whom I cheated and deceived. I re-travelled the roads over mountains and crossed rivers during my young adult years. The light in my soul diminished and departed from my body. My body had died but my spirit returned.

There wasn't much of a gathering at the crematorium as the incense smoke spiralled into the hot air. My family couldn't come due to distance and the fact I was cremated only three days after passing away. The monks whom I had taught when living in Sihanoukville performed the ceremony. An image of myself and one of the Buddha along with flowers and fruit surrounded my casket. Finally, the wheel of life and death had gone full circle and both our spirits could go our separate ways.

In the dream, Don, Duka, and Roza stood behind the monks. The little girl's spirit wasn't present. I had always assumed she was a curse and that some form of adversity or misfortune had befallen or attached itself to me since meeting her. I understood otherwise now, she had let her killer live, knowing that Karma was paying him back by suffering excruciating pain in his old age.

.oOo.

I suddenly awoke with sweat running down my back. It was time for me to work hard and gather merit. I would clear up matters here in Kampot and then return to the Temple in Sihanoukville.

I had kept a diary since my arrival in Cambodia.

I stood by the river edge naked as the day I was born. I tore page by page from my book and threw them into the water. I watched them drift off into the distance. I then plunged myself into the water although there is no baptism in Buddhist tradition, I felt the urge to cleanse myself. I wasn't going to be attached anymore to my past.

It was a new chapter in my life and a fresh new start. I was no longer going to run away from my life but instead would run towards all the good deeds that I could do. After all, I had to do my part to make the world a better place for children like little Aisha.

ACKNOWLEDGEMENTS

I would like to thank the Future Pathways team for their support and putting me in touch with the Book Whisperers. I would also like to give a special thanks to Mary Turner Thomson of The Book Whisperers, who guided me step by step to edit the book. I appreciate your help advice and direction.

www.future-pathways.co.uk
www.thebookwhisperers.com

Printed in Great Britain
by Amazon